STOLEN PIECES III
Hidden Darkness

Copyright ©2024 by J.R. Mason
All rights reserved. No part of this publication may be reproduced, stored, or transmitted in any form or by any means without prior written consent from the author.

This is a work of fiction. Any similarities to other people or events are purely coincidental.

Cover design: J. René Creative
Editor: *Eloquently Edited* by Kim
Back cover headshot: David Paige

To Rafael Burgos, you are missed beyond words. #RWG

To my amazingly dedicated readers, thank you for your support. Hoping you don't get lost in the darkness. If for any reason your mental health should decline after this read, blame the characters – I just wrote their crazy shit down.

Content Warnings:

Sexual Assault/Abuse, Domestic Violence, Psychological Torture, Strong Language, Sexual Situations, Drug Usage, Abduction

1

In his late wife's Mercedes-Benz Sportster with fully tinted windows, Weston sat filled to the brim with rage and hostility, staring up at the giant window that spanned the entire floor of the apartment. He watched the woman he once adored, the detective who shattered his heart and destroyed every piece of him emotionally, stare out that window at the movement of the city below her. He smiled as she winced in pain, trying her best to pull her hair into a ponytail, but her shoulder injury was making that extremely difficult. She eventually gave up on the up-do and retreated from the window.

His eyes caught a familiar, well-dressed agent exiting the building, taking keys from the valet with a smile, sliding into his car, and speeding off. Weston's gloved hand lightly stroked the stolen Glock on his passenger seat as he scanned the area taking note of all the visible cameras, in addition to the ones that would only be identifiable to the trained eye.

He noticed an entry point in the back alley - one that the service members and staff frequently used. Oddly enough, it didn't appear to have surveillance coverage. He had just assumed that this expensive and upscale complex would be impenetrable without somehow being caught on video. He thought *I should just go handle her right now. I could go in, shoot her with his gun, and leave it to look like he did it.* Fuck! *He doesn't have an actual motive. Plus, he's FBI. He wouldn't just shoot her in his house and leave. That just screams "I was framed." Not to mention, after that incident with the mayor...* Conrad hadn't been formally charged with anything yet and he happened to know, firsthand, that she still wanted Claudia dead. *I could just do it and collect the fee. But a death that quick would be* way *too good for that unscrupulous bitch. I want to make her suffer. I want them* both *to suffer. I want to* hurt *her and fuck every thought of him out of her head. She was mine. She still is. Just be patient.*

On his reckless drive home, Weston thought about everything that had transpired between them over the last year and a half. Prior to her attack, they were so good together – a loving and affectionate pair. She was all the things that his wife was not. Then, out of nowhere, she just seemed to have changed. She stopped behaving like his sweet Claudy and became bolder, feistier, and more aggressive. Weston understood how trauma had the power to change a person though. Look at *him*.

He caught his reflection in Alli's clean tinted windows as he exited her tiny granite-colored vehicle - one that not many people knew about because she didn't drive it frequently. He observed his overgrown, disheveled, salt-

and-pepper beard - a far cry from his usual clean-cut appearance. His dark, untamed hair that hadn't been cut in a month of Sundays did nothing to help improve his overall look. The redness in his eyes could have simply been metaphorical rage, but more likely due to the drinking and many tears shed because of his current situation. He was on a leave of absence after brutally murdering his pregnant wife to gain custody of his children so that he could be with the love of his life... who was *literally* in another man's bed. The sounds of Maceo driving into Claudia in her kitchen that night replayed in his mind like Satan's punishment. He couldn't stop hearing the screams of her physical betrayal or thinking about it, which only served to make him even more furious. In the month since Alessandra's "accident," he had been taking his hostile feelings out on the weights in their state-of-the-art, in-home gym, lifting in fury and resentment multiple times per day, getting stronger... until the opportunity would present itself to take it out on the detective instead.

2

The typically bustling squad room was eerily quiet for a change. Detective Jonas Torrey sat motionless at his desk listening to the air enter and exit his tense body. It was his first day back to work since his fiancée Brenna was gunned down by his colleague. He was still having trouble wrapping his mind around why she was there in the first place. He had gone through her phone for any clues as to why and found a call history with Lainey. But their text messages were so vague that he couldn't make much from them in terms of her reason. He stared despondently at Lainey's desk. The room wasn't the same without her bubbly personality always joking around, and always being nosy up in someone's business.

He breathed deeply as his eyes shifted to Maceo's desk, formerly occupied by the late Detective Tanner Lockhart, neither of whom was on the team any longer.

His eyes narrowed as they made their way to Claudia's desk. A laundry list of people was dead, and she seemed to be in the center of all the chaos and despair. Torrey exhaled slowly as he thought about his colleague and Alessandra and how their daughter would grow up never knowing her parents. After the official DNA results came back, she was placed with her father's family. They named her after both of her parents, Tanner Alessia Lockhart.

He strolled over to Lainey's desk and began rummaging through to see if he could find any clues as to why Brenna was there that night. He picked up the small notepad she often scribbled in when he was startled from behind.

"Hey, man," Burgess said with a pat on his shoulder before making his way to his desk.

Torrey jumped slightly, then exhaled.

"Sorry. Didn't mean to scare you."

"Nah, you're good. Just uhh… Just surprised they haven't packed up Lainey's stuff yet."

"Yeah…" Burgess agreed, taking a seat. "I'm sure they will soon because I think some people are transferring in, and Officer Denise Rainer just made Detective."

"Wait, she's the one with the big…"

"Yup," Burgess interrupted, not needing Torrey to finish the question.

"Hmmm," Torrey nodded.

"She made detective pretty quick. Makes ya wonder how," Burgess said suggestively.

"Now you know damn well," Torrey interjected, "This is where Lainey would do a literal *swan* dive into your ass and accuse you of being a sexist dick," he chuckled. "*Just because a woman has tits the size of someone's head doesn't mean she's using them to get ahead*," he joked, mocking his late colleague.

Burgess laughed, shaking his head. "Yeah, you're right, man."

He got up and approached Torrey who was still leaning against the side of Lainey's desk. "So, what about you?" he asked genuinely. "How you holdin' up?"

"I mean, I'm here. But I'm not okay." Torrey looked down at his shoes as he continued speaking. "I was ready to spend my life with that woman. I don't know how I'm supposed to just get over this and move on."

Burgess nodded, unsure of what words were even helpful at that moment.

"Her uhhh... her wedding gown arrived the other day," Torrey continued. "She was wild," he whispered with a nostalgic grin, shaking his head and then wiping a stray tear that formed at the thought of her. "You know my girl had a *black* wedding gown custom-made!?"

"No wayyy!"

"Yeah... She was about to surprise everyone there - even me! I had no idea. I just wanted a black-on-black winter wedding, but I just assumed she'd still wear some shade of white, but... You know Brenna. Always the trendsetter and going against the grain. What I loved so much about her," he added sadly. "And how about she'd ordered Cairo a cubic zirconia studded collar and leash so he could look just as fresh walkin' her down the aisle," he lightly chuckled.

"Black Doberman... Black-tie affair... Black... *people*," Burgess joked, trying to lift his friend's spirits. "That wedding woulda been sexy as hell. I'm just... really sorry, man."

"Thanks," he replied, sliding Lainey's small notepad into his back pocket once Burgess turned away.

"Guys! My office, now!" Captain Higgins bellowed.

Torrey and Burgess walked in and took seats opposite the captain.

"Good to have you back, Torrey. Your absence was definitely felt."

"I see. We're really short-staffed here."

"Not for long. Burgess may have told you that Officer Rainer will be joining us... well, *Detective* now. And I'm still interviewing for the other slot. I've gotta get on top of getting those desks cleaned out," Higgins said with a note of sadness in his voice. "Also," he paused, "Martinez should be back by next week."

Torrey's entire expression and demeanor shifted. "You can't be serious, Cap? She shot the love of my life!"

"And I'm sorry about that, I really am. But Internal Affairs is still investigating the accident, so she hasn't been formally charged..."

"Again..." Torrey sighed. "Okay, she shot Lockhart - he attacked her. But Brenna was innocent."

"And it was an *accident*," Higgins interrupted. "Her gun went off when Lainey shot her... Sadly, Brenna was just in the wrong place at the wrong time."

"Which, that shit is crazy as fuck too! You really believe this? Lainey was the most empathetic person alive! Not to mention she's like 125 pounds soaking wet! Yeah, she's a badass, but there's no way she's abducting grown-ass men over double her weight *and* dismembering them! Come on! Please tell me you're not just lettin' this shit slide, Cap!"

"Torrey, what do you want me to do? The evidence was collected, Internal Affairs investigated, and the victims' items were located inside Lainey's password-protected safe in the back of her closet. She quite *literally* had *stolen pieces* in more ways than one! I will run with it if you can give me another logical explanation. I promise I will. But if not, there's nothing else I can do."

The room fell silent because everyone knew he was correct. Without additional evidence that would clearly refute the current evidence, what else could possibly be done?

The pair listened quietly, but in disbelief, as the captain disclosed the entire Maceo situation and how he was FBI undercover investigating their stolen pieces investigation.

"Wow," Torrey muttered. "Just... Fuckin' *wow!*"

"Calm down. It was not about us and our abilities, but more about locating the insider who was disassembling people before that person could get to the witness."

"And Dr. Berardi is dead. Clearly, that didn't work," Burgess grumbled.

"So, if Lainey is this alleged insider," Torrey snipped, "That would imply that she's the one who killed the M.E. which was impossible because we were all still at her engagement party. She ran out of her *own* party when she heard about the accident and left us there! *Come on*, Cap!

You can't just let this slide! It makes no logical sense! I don't know who did it, but one thing for sure, two things for certain, it *wasn't* Lainey!"

3

Tossing and turning, unable to sleep, Ruby lay in the bed staring through the darkness, listening to Maceo breathe heavily beside her. She was jealous of his peaceful slumber that she was unable to enter into because she had so much on her mind. She had accepted payments in full to take out three other monsters, but she couldn't possibly engage in such activities with the limited strength and mobility in her arm. That nebby bitch Lainey shooting her threw everything off. She had already planned how she was going to eliminate Kelly Knight, who had presented her home as a loving environment, taking in fosters, who usually needed longer-term placement. When Children and Youth Services removed a little girl from her father's home, who shouldn't have been taken, the six-year-old was returned to her father completely traumatized. The girl accused Kelly of not feeding her and locking her in the room all day, every day. She was pocketing the foster stipend and living her best life, not using it to care for the children who were placed with her. CYS received the father's angry complaint and scheduled a visit to the home. But of course, everything would be perfect during a scheduled visit. Nothing came of his complaint; the neglectful woman was still taking in fosters, and the fact that his daughter was returned to him a completely different child from when she was mistakenly removed in the first place infuriated him. Kelly was next on her list before the whole shooting drama transpired.

Ruby quietly lifted herself from the bed, walked over to the enormous window, and slid the thick blackout curtain open slightly so she could peek out at the sleeping city below. Those thick drapes were a necessary evil, as Downtown Pittsburgh was the total antithesis of her residential situation. She could sleep with her curtains wide open, and nothing but darkness and tranquility would spill in through her open windows. But downtown, the bright yellow lights that lined the sidewalks wouldn't sleep until morning. The illuminated bridge to the left reflected off the murky Allegheny River. And so many headlights. Why were so many people on the road still at one o'clock in the morning Downtown where very little was open on a weeknight? She looked up at the half-moon, barely visible through the city's smog and cloudy skies, and thought about how much she missed home. Her mind drifted back to the issue at hand. Should she return the money? Or maybe she could instruct them on how to do it themselves and make it look accidental? She thought to herself, *give a woman a fish, she can eat for a day. Teach a woman to murder people, she can kill for a lifetime... or however the saying goes.*

"Baby, you okay?" a groggy voice questioned from the king-size bed.

When she glanced back, she noticed him squinting because of how much light cut through the pitch-blackness of the bedroom.

"I'm sorry. I have a lot on my mind and was just thinking," she answered.

Maceo's eyes ran up her curvy body, silhouetted by the outside light coming through the enormous window. "Naked thinkin' huh? Is it workin'?" he asked, sliding his sheets aside and stepping out of the bed to approach her. "I need to think too... I think," he joked, pressing his nude body against hers and wrapping his arms around her waist as they both quietly stared down at the desolate sidewalks and parked cars.

"You do realize that we ain't that far up right? Anyone paying close enough attention's gonna see this stunning body of yours that you've placed on display, that I don't know that I care to share," he whispered in her ear, running his strong hands up her stomach, over her breasts, then gliding his middle finger across her neck.

She let out a starved moan as she slowly ground her thick cheeks into his pelvis repeatedly until he began to stiffen against her. They hadn't had sex since before her accident and her body, despite the pain and trauma, was screaming to feel him deep inside of her.

"Uhhhh," he moaned, wanting it just as badly as she did, but he moved his hands to her hips to stop her wanton gyrations.

"Baby, I- are you sure? I don't want to hurt you," he expressed, looking at the scar from the through-and-through gunshot wound on the back of her shoulder just below her collarbone and all the bruising around it, in addition to the yellowish bruising across her upper back that was trying to heal. It just looked painful to him. "I don't mind waiting. I'll wait for you."

Ruby turned around and softly exhaled when she leaned her back against the window's cool glass. Maceo wasn't wrong. Her upper body was still very sore, but that didn't stop her lower half from aching for him. She stared into his eyes and subtly scratched her neck from the itchy tingles that she hated so much.

"Detective... Excuse me, *Agent* James," she said, scanning his perfectly structured face that held so much genuine concern for her well-being. "While I admire your restraint and truly appreciate your care for me," her gaze darkened, "I would have fucked you in that hospital bed weeks ago - right there in front of that simpleton Bradley Pitt," she said, imitating his southern accent. "If you hadn't noticed, Agent, I find certain types of pain quite pleasurable," Ruby admitted, pinching her hardened nipples. "So, are you going to make me pleasure *myself*, or are you going to help a sista out?"

Maceo smacked her already bruised hands away from her nipples and hungrily took them into his mouth one by one. She moaned desperately as he slid his other hand up her inner thigh to find that an entire waterfall of her essence awaited him. He was taken aback because she had been shot and had major surgery not too long ago, yet her body was able to completely disregard that and ready itself for his visitation.

She gyrated her pelvis into his fingers softly begging, "Please" which typically wasn't in her nature.

Kissing up her neck and making his way to her lips, he murmured, "I love it when you beg," before hungrily attacking her mouth with his. She kept begging please in between kisses because all she wanted was him inside of her.

Maceo turned her around in a manner that to any average person would appear rough, but for their usual style of sex, that was pretty gentle. He ran his fingers up through the base of her long, straightened hair, forcefully lifting it from her neck where he planted kisses across her bruised back as she moaned in pleasure from his continued manual stimulation.

With his hand still tightly grasping her hair at the root, Mace lifted her leg and easily slid into her from behind with a guttural growl. He plowed into her with a more controlled kind of aggression that wouldn't hurt Ruby further but was nowhere close to what would be considered lovemaking. She cried out in ecstasy as he stretched her out while focused on her love button with one hand and still tugging on her hair with the other.

From the gray car with the tinted windows, Weston watched Claudia's face contort in pleasure, her thick, naked body pressed against the window, putting their filth on display for all of Pittsburgh.

He was fuming but couldn't stop watching as he stroked his growing erection through his pants. It wasn't long ago when they sat in the Fairmont Hotel, and he requested that *they* get a room and make love just like that in front of the window. Claudia had declined his request, yet there she was fucking this guy in the window of his home. As far as he was concerned, *he* should be the one inside of her. *He* should be stroking her into ecstasy, not sitting in his car touching his own dick.

In the throes of the massive orgasm Ruby was finally having, she barely noticed when the Mercedes Sportster loudly and recklessly peeled out of the parking spot across the five-lane street.

Weston arrived home and immediately went to peek in on the boys. He knew damn well he shouldn't have been leaving them alone at night to watch a woman who clearly didn't want him. But he was unraveling and couldn't help himself.

The twins were still soundly asleep, so he made his way to the master bathroom, immediately stripped down, and hopped into a cool shower for some sexual relief. He slowly stroked himself while fantasizing about Claudia's phenomenal oral skills. He flashed back to their illicit daytime sex on her deck. But it wasn't until he fantasized about angrily driving into her with his sturdy hands squeezed tightly around her neck until her eyes glassed over that he finally released. Breathing heavily but feeling a little better, he washed up, threw on a pair of boxers, and immediately fell asleep.

4

Cairo's head quickly lifted from his sleeping position when he heard his dad, Detective Jonas Torrey amble out of his bedroom and into the living room. He plopped down onto the couch with a long exhale, so Cairo immediately ran over for some good morning lovins.

"Hey, boyyy. G'mornin," he said with a weak smile as he gave the large canine scratches and pets. Cairo sat staring up at him with the most expressive brown eyes that Jonas was convinced could see straight into his soul. He rested his heavy head on Jonas' thigh and let out a barely audible whimper.

"You miss her, huh?" He paused as though they were having a legit conversation. "Yeah, me too."

On the coffee table, he noticed Lainey's pocket notepad, which he had stolen from her desk. Finally taking the time to flip through it, he saw that there were only random case notes about recent crime scenes and mentions of Dr. Berardi's car accident, even though they were not assigned to that case. Other than that, there was nothing out of the ordinary. That is until he found some scribbles of Cairo's name and vague info about cadaver dogs. When he flipped the page, there was a strange drawing, but there were no words to indicate where or what this diagram was.

"What were you and Mama gettin' into?" he asked the dog, still stroking that spot he loved behind his ears.

After a few more minutes of relaxing head scratches, Cairo darted away and then returned, clumsily dragging his leash. Jonas couldn't help but laugh when he dropped it in front of him and barked, loudly demanding to leave the house.

"Okay, buddy I got you," he chuckled. "You go out and pee while I get dressed, and we'll go for a ride," Jonas offered, sliding open the glass door for Cairo to exit.

The couple didn't live too far from Raccoon State Park, where Brenna used to take him onto the lake to train him in water remains detection. From what Jonas gathered, she would go out onto the lake, leave a small sample, return for Cairo, and ride around the lake until he gave his signal. But what Jonas didn't know was how Cairo handled the detections. Since he was already sitting with his head leaned over the edge of the canoe, he would tap his large paws and then lay down to indicate that something, or *someone*, was in that area of the water. In a real-life situation, Brenna would then notify the police and the dive team of where they should be looking to find their victim. Every time she made that call, somebody was pulled out of the water. Jonas couldn't deny how impressive that dog was. But he also couldn't help but wonder where she got the remains from and how she got them back out of the water. Did she ever get them out of the water? He kayaked in that water. Add it to the growing list of things he should have asked her when he had the chance, but he thought he had more time.

Ninety-seven pounds of muscular excitement did his best to wait patiently while Jonas parked the car for their walk. Admittedly, he didn't do this as often as he should have. He and Brenna would come out together sometimes to walk Cairo down one of his favorite trails, but he rarely spent one-on-one time with her big baby.

Toward the end of their walk, his thoughts of Bren and why she and Cairo were in Lainey's notebook were interrupted by a call from the captain, asking if he could stop in.

"C'mon boy, let's go," Jonas said as he began to jog the trail. Cairo was right there easily keeping up with him for a few minutes, until he abruptly stopped, causing Jonas to almost stumble when the leash halted him.

"Ayyye dude! What the hell!?" he yelled, walking back toward the dog.

Breathing heavily, he watched a panting Cairo take a seat.

"What's the matter?" Jonas asked, also heaving. "I'm tired too, but we gotta go," he said, turning to walk away, but Cairo stayed.

"Look. *You're* supposed to be in better shape than *me*. Come on, let's move!"

Another jogger ran past and yelled, "Beautiful dog, man!"

"Yeah, thanks!" he nodded back.

"Can we go now?"

Cairo weighed as much as a small human. And Jonas was only weighing in at about 70 pounds more than the dog, so if he didn't want to move, good luck. After a few more attempts, Cairo finally got up and slowly followed Jonas back to the car.

When the glass doors swung open at the precinct, Torrey might as well have been invisible because all anyone in the room saw was the dog. He couldn't help but wonder if this was how Brenna felt every time she stepped out with him.

"Heyyy, Buddyyyy!" Cairo's butt excitedly wiggled back and forth as he accepted all the love from Torrey's colleagues.

"Y'all know I'm here too, right?" he said, shaking his head.

"Yeah yeah," Rookie Detective Denise Rainer joked. "You want us to come pet you too?"

"Funny," Torrey replied, unleashing Cairo, because he didn't need one. His behavior and listening skills were impeccable. "Running in to see Cap right quick."

As the stately canine made his rounds through the squad room to collect head scratches, his nose was in everybody's business, taking in the various scents. He sniffed his way over and then immediately sat down, facing the desk that adjoined Det. Rainer beside the panoramic window. Cairo didn't move except to turn his head to look at the other team members, then turned in the other direction to look for his dad. But he just sat, visually examining the desk area.

Torrey exited the office and noticed Cairo seated with his back to the squad, staring straight ahead. He called him as he strolled over to his colleagues. Cairo looked over at him but didn't move a muscle.

"The hell did y'all do to my dog? I was gone for four minutes."

"C'mon Cai, let's go!" he tried once more.

Still unconcerned with the instructions given to him, Cairo sat until Torrey went over to reattach his leash. He whimpered before finally giving in and leaving that spot.

Burgess stopped them. "Yo, that shit is crazy," he whispered. "How he just sat at Martinez's desk like that? You think he knows?"

"Do I think my dog knows that the person who belongs to that desk, who hasn't even been here for a month, shot his mom? Seriously?"

"He was there, right?"

"Yeah, but he was up the hill in the car."

"I mean, Brenna once told me this dog can find dead people - that are underwater!" Burgess shrugged at Torrey as if to ask, are you stupid, man?

They both looked down at Cairo who looked back up at them.

"Well, what does he do when he finds what he's looking for?"

"I don't know. I thought Bren said he'd lie down or something."

"Hmmm... I don't know then," Burgess commented. "But that was definitely weird."

Ruby rested in the darkness, waiting for Maceo's breathing to deepen, indicating that he was well into a sound sleep. She had no choice but to add a little something extra to his wine at dinner so that she could get out of the house and handle this job. She felt mildly guilty about the number of times she had done that, but she needed to know what some of these people's nightly routines were, and she knew she would be questioned if she tried to just leave in the middle of the night, especially with a healing gunshot wound. This was way easier when she lived alone in a secluded location, where she could come and go as she pleased - and the world was none the wiser. This cohabitation bullshit was complicating everything.

She got dressed as quickly as she could with her bum arm that still tingled and went numb periodically from the nerve damage. She pulled back her hair as best she could, switched her phone to silent, and then plugged it into the charger by the bed.

On her way out, she took Maceo's keys instead of her own, snuck down through the back to the garage, and drove off into the night to handle the next person on her list. With that trashy woman's history, Ruby had come up with a brilliant idea.

Just before midnight, Ruby carefully crept through the darkness down the back between the homes. At this point, the easiest way to get someone to pull over or open their doors for her was to simply use the one tool she'd never even considered. Of course, she could use her badge to gain access to this woman's home at night because she wasn't going to live to tell the tale. It was so brilliant that she was immediately annoyed she hadn't considered that option much sooner. All that running people down with high beams and whatnot when all she needed to do was use the red and blue flashing light she'd purchased for her car to pull them over. It was fun, though - scaring the hell out of them. But now, with her temporary disability, she needed to be able to get the job done in the easiest possible manner.

The light from the television illuminated the living room when she knocked on the door.

"Who is it!?" the woman belligerently screamed. "And why the fuck are you at my door this late?" she mumbled under her breath, but Ruby still heard it.

"Pittsburgh P.D." Ruby replied, knocking loudly once more to force urgency.

The door briskly swung open to reveal a disheveled woman glancing out past Ruby to see what was going on outside. Because why else would the police be bothering her at this hour? But all was quiet and peaceful on the block.

"What's going on?" she asked.

"Ms. Knight, I'm Officer... Lainey Crane. Children and Youth Services sent me for a surprise visit," she replied, holding up a clipboard with some papers affixed to it.

The woman immediately looked down at the cigarette dangling between her fingers that she was not supposed to be smoking in the house, per CYS rules. "Sure. Sorry. Come on in."

So focused on the fact that this was even happening, Kelly never even noticed that when Ruby flashed her shield and held up the clipboard, her hands were covered with the infamous black nitrile gloves.

She was granted access to the home, and looking around, she wondered how this hot mess ever passed any sort of inspection. This was not an environment fit for anyone's child. Did CYS even come? Or was this woman so nasty that she could only keep it clean for a few days at a time?

Taking a seat with her at the dining room table, Ruby asked, "Do you have children in your care currently?"

"No. One just left, but I have another coming tomorrow afternoon."

"Perfect," she replied with a sadistic glint in her eyes.

6

Ruby strolled into the Steamy Bean on her first day back to work. Admittedly, it was a little weird doing it without Lainey. But if it meant she still had her freedom as a result of silencing her, she was fine with that. It was also refreshing to order her coffee without her little pervert's eyes on her. She knew she would need something strong and black, other than Maceo, because, given the nature of her injury, she would again, likely be placed on some form of light duty.

Fortunately, she was able to follow someone in through the precinct doors. Carrying her work bag over her good shoulder and two coffees with the same hand, she would have struggled to pull the heavy door open with her other arm.

"Baby faaaace!" a deep but jolly voice echoed through the lobby. He always had some pet name for her and Lainey that many women may have felt offended or belittled by, but they didn't feel like he had any ill intent. He was a genuine sweetheart.

"Hey, Teddy!" Ruby smiled, setting down his black coffee with two creams and one sugar. "Gotcha something good."

"*And* you remembered my name this time," he laughed heartily, recalling when she came back the last time she'd called him Theodore, a name he'd only heard from his parents when he was in big trouble.

"I see you got jokes today," she chuckled.

"For you, always! I missed ya! How you holding up?" he asked, his cheeks still red from the earlier laughter.

"Okay." *Time to turn on this empathy and sorrow bullshit.* "It's been rough..."

"I bet. Crane was something else. It's just so hard to believe she was involved in something that crazy."

Ruby narrowed her eyes and asked, "Why?"

"Sweet, bubbly, goofy Lainey? At least monthly, she would come through this lobby with a spider or some form of insect in a clear cup to escort it back outside. She wouldn't even step on a bug, but we're to believe that she just... dismembered actual people?"

"Teddy, I don't think you realize how many people there are in this world who can watch a movie where eighteen people are violently slaughtered, but if that dog were to even accidentally be harmed, they're goin' off! Throw the whole damn movie away."

"Yeah, I guess you're right," he nodded. "I met who I assume will be your new partner. She's no Crane, though."

Good. I don't need those problems.

"Welcome back," Torrey said tersely.

"Thank you," Ruby replied, setting down her things.

"How's the shoulder?" he asked dryly.

"Getting there," she lied, not intending to tell anyone about the nerve damage that would have her at a desk longer than she'd like.

Torrey nodded. "Good. Now that all the small talk bullshit is outta the way, tell me why exactly my fiancée was at your house that late at night," he demanded, staring daggers at Claudia.

"Torrey-" the captain interjected as he briskly strolled toward them.

He boldly put his hand up as if to stop him from any further interruptions, his nostrils flaring.

Ruby looked around and noticed all the attention shift to them as Burgess and the new detective she hadn't even met yet looked on. "Can we go somewhere else and discuss this privately? Everyone is watching."

"I don't give a fuck about these people. Answer my question!" he huffed more forcefully.

"Torrey, Internal Affairs has alread-"

"I don't give a fuck about them *either*," he angrily hissed at Higgins, his eyes never departing from Claudia's.

Who the hell does this little idiot think he's talking to? Ruby chuckled to herself. *That's fine. I will tell this whole squad room a story that makes me sound even more like the victim. Thank you, little idiot, for this perfect platform to share my harrowing tale of woe.*

"Okay, well..." she glanced around nervously and picked at her cuticles just as Claudia would. "I believe Lainey was the one who was watching me. I found a small walking path leading from the open end of my woods to the area near my house. Someone had walked it many times. I'm guessing it was her? Why else would she be out at my house that late?"

"Get to the point. Why was my fiancée with her?"

"She wasn't. It was just Lainey... at first. I caught her, and she drew her weapon, so I drew mine. Once she mentioned Tanner, I knew she would eventually fire because why would she tell me all that and leave me alive?"

Torrey stared at her like he was going to rip out her damn tongue if she didn't answer the question.

"During our back and forth, someone came down the hill behind Lainey, but it was dark. I couldn't tell who it was. Lainey must not have known that she was there either because you don't just shoot someone in cold blood... and leave witnesses," Ruby added to cast suspicion. "My finger was already on the trigger but when the bullet hit me, I guess the way I spun with my finger pulling the trigger too, my weapon fired, hitting who I later found out was Brenna. Then Maceo showed up."

Torrey's eyes began to pool with tears as he furrowed his brow.

"I'm so sorry, Jonas. It all just happened so fast, but she was still moving after she fell. I was down, but I could hear her crying out and the leaves beneath her crunching," Ruby lied, knowing damn well she fired with precision and delivered a perfect kill shot.

"What are you saying, Claudia?" he asked, still holding back tears.

Ruby sighed. "Lainey was the one who went to check her vitals. *She* was the one who announced that Brenna was gone. But... she stood over her much longer than it took to take a pulse." *Check.*

Silence crept across the room.

Ruby continued, "It only takes what? Five seconds or so?"

More silence.

"After Lainey shot me, and Mace ran to get help, she tried to *smother* me, which is why I shot her. That one was not an accident, but Brenna *absolutely* was. So, to answer your question, I'm not sure *why* she was there, but I am *so* sorry this happened," she expressed in a tone so sincere and anguished that they could feel everyone in the room exhale. Then she considered, *If this police thing ends up not working out for any reason, I can always pursue a career in acting.*

Torrey shifted his eyes downward which caused the puddles of pain to stroll down his cheeks.

The room was so quiet for a moment; it was like everyone stopped breathing altogether. *Checkmate.* Ruby smirked on the inside.

"Torrey. My office. *Now!*" the captain yelled, angrily destroying the silence.

The rest of the team watched the captain's door close, and his shades draw immediately thereafter.

Torrey instantly launched into an apology. "Cap, I'm sorry... I- I just couldn't help it. I needed answers that no one else was giving me," he said remorsefully.

"Are you good now?" he asked, taking a seat.

"Yes, sir," Torrey replied, composing himself.

"Is this, the two of you, going to be a problem?"

"No, sir."

"Fine. Carry on, then."

7

"Not exactly the best first impression," Ruby chuckled to Detective Denise Rainer. She extended her arm for a handshake. "But nice to meet you finally."

"You as well," Rainer agreed. "I've heard amazing things about you - well, other than the... you know."

"Yeah," she quickly replied.

While Ruby literally woke up thinking about having a man inside of her body, she couldn't deny Detective Denise Rainer had a certain je ne sais quoi. It wasn't just her enormous breasts that they had all heard so much about before she'd arrived, but more her bad-bitch kind of swag. One didn't need to see the helmet sitting on the desk to know she rode a motorcycle to work that morning. Her flawless, dark chocolate skin naturally glowed alongside her glossy, perfectly shaped lips that looked like she had just left the surgeon's office, but in reality, those were probably her real lips. She wasn't wearing any makeup other than the clear lip gloss, but somehow, her dark eyes still popped.

Torrey exited the captain's office with him not far behind.

"Alright," Higgins announced. "Firstly, Martinez! Great to have you back. You met Rainer?"

She nodded.

"Okay, good. Train her up right."

"And try not to shoot her," Torrey mumbled under his breath.

Ohhh... You're gonna pay for that one.

"Torrey!" Higgins yelled. "Look," he said, gripping his thick graying hair. "What happened was a tragedy. But we have to work together. I need us to be a team. You said this was not going to be a problem," he directed at Torrey.

"It's not. I'm good. *Sorry*," he said to Claudia like a petulant child being forced to apologize to his sibling.

She nodded in acceptance.

"Alright. Police are on the scene on the North Side. A woman was found dead in her home. Kelly Knight. Here's the information," he said, handing the file to Detective Torrey. "Take Rainer with you."

"Cap, we're not doing this again. Let me at least ride along?" Ruby insisted.

He glanced over at Torrey who was rolling his eyes. "Fine. Ride along so you can fix this shit here," he said, pointing between the two of them. "But don't *touch* shit... don't *do* shit. You are *literally* just riding along today."

"Perfect, thanks," she said, grabbing her navy-blue Pittsburgh Police jacket.

Once they made it to the cruiser, Ruby, as the more senior team member, naturally went to take the front seat.

"No," Torrey firmly objected. "Rainer, take shotgun. *You* are only riding along, remember? You heard the captain."

She exhaled. *Keep your cool.* "Fine."

"Sorry," Rainer whispered sympathetically.

"It's okay," Ruby said, sliding into the back seat.

As they pulled up to Kelly Knight's home, surrounded by police, neighbors, and crime scene tape, Ruby struggled to figure out why they were even there. That was all she could think about the entire ride over.

When they entered the home and made their way to the kitchen, Laura was on the scene photographing everything, including the open tequila bottle on the table where Kelly had been seated, along with the mostly empty glass. As they approached the victim, Dr. Kathryn Hale stood to greet them. She had been Alessandra's assistant and was recently promoted to the freshly vacant position of medical examiner. "Claudia! So glad to see you're well and back with us."

"Thank you, Kathryn. Have you met our new addition, Detective Denise Rainer?"

"I have! It's good to see you again. And you as well, Detective Torrey."

They all noted the body of 57-year-old Kelly Knight lying on the floor with a gash on her forehead. There was also blood on the edge of the table, as though she had hit her head when she'd fallen forward and then out of the chair.

"I'm a little confused as to why you called us. There's a tourniquet around her upper arm and a needle. It clearly looks like she overdosed here," Torrey remarked.

Ruby was glad he said it because she didn't want to draw any attention to herself. She just wanted to know what *they* knew as early as possible.

The new Medical Examiner kneeled beside the body, "Yes, she did overdose. But this was not self-inflicted."

Ruby's breath hitched. *How the fuck could she possibly know that? I was flawless.*

Dr. Hale waited before speaking to see if the detectives saw what she'd observed.

"Ohhh daaaamn…" Rainer moaned, finally detecting it.

Ruby noticed as well and immediately felt sick to her stomach. *How the fuck could I overlook something that basic? If I hadn't missed this one simple thing, police would've walked in, it would have been ruled an overdose, and that would have been that. Fuck!*

"It looks like she shot up in her left arm like most people would, but her watch is on her right arm, which means she's likely left-handed. So, she would have shot up in the other arm."

Ruby's breathing staggered, so she stepped away to conceal it. *Fuck!*

"Exactly," Dr. Hale agreed.

"Also, based on her height and where this chair is positioned in relation to the table, there's no way her head would have hit the edge here had she fallen forward. This entire scene was staged," Torrey noted.

"Plus, had she simply been sitting in this chair drinking when she allegedly overdosed and fell forward to hit the table, there's not enough force to cause this deep of a gash," Kathryn explained. "She might have had a small knot at most. So, the assailant either slammed her head into this table or delivered the injury another way and added the blood there to make it appear as though she fell forward and hit her head."

Ruby's mind was spinning, which made the room feel like it was spinning as well, but in the opposite direction. She could not get her thoughts together because never in a million years should she have been that sloppy. If she hadn't already killed Lainey, she'd be ready to kill her now. This is *all* her fault. Had she minded her own damn business, everyone would still be alive right now, and her brain wouldn't be total mush from those long-term effects of the anesthesia from the surgery and all the drugs she was on.

"Once I get her back to the lab, I'll be able to test to find out what was in that syringe and if she really *did* drink what was in that bottle or if it was just planted there for appearance's sake."

"Thanks, Dr. Hale." Torrey glanced up at Martinez. "Well, this is new. Nothing to say?"

Ruby gathered herself and shook her head no. "I'm just riding along, remember?"

Upon entering his home, Jonas was met with immediate demands for affection. He could barely set his Chinese takeout on the counter before he was lovingly bombarded.

Seated alone, with only the background noise of the television to keep him company, Jonas stared across the table at the empty seat that Brenna used to occupy. He couldn't stop thinking about what Claudia had said about Lainey, and if she really was capable of hurting Brenna. The assumption was that the gunshot wound killed her. He would have never considered that she was still alive afterward and finished off by someone else, let alone someone he trusted. It seemed so hard to believe. But the best killers are, of course, the ones people would never suspect.

His attention was pulled from those thoughts by the news story that came on.

The body of a missing 31-year-old Hopewell man, Jamie Darlington, has been located this afternoon.

He immediately jumped up and grabbed the remote to increase the volume.

Emergency dispatchers told Pittsburgh's Action News 4 the body was found in a wooded area off the trails in Racoon State Park. Township police say preliminary information does indicate signs of foul play. The victim was taken to the Beaver County Medical Examiner's Office for further investigation to determine the cause of death. Be sure to stay with us as we learn more on this tragic story.

Jonas stood in front of the television with his mouth hanging open, then shifted his eyes to Cairo, who was lying in his enormous bed with one paw draped over his stuffed octopus.

"Cairo!" he yelled, causing his head to pop up. "What the hell, my guy!? You knew that man was there days ago!" he exclaimed, shaking his head. Jonas wasn't sure why he was so shocked since that was literally what he did for fun. But he just wasn't expecting to see it play out in everyday life, doing mundane activities like taking a jog.

Jonas was slowly realizing that all of Cairo's training was going to waste. He either needed to learn how to handle this dog for detection purposes or get him to someone who could. But he also knew that Brenna would haunt him for the rest of his days if he were to rehome her baby.

Taking a seat on the couch, Cairo approached Jonas with his octopus dangling from his mouth, looking like an oversized puppy. "So every time you start chillin' I'm gonna find a body? Seriously?"

Cairo just stared up at him, squeaking the stuffed toy once.

"So how am I supposed to know if you're just tired or someone's dead? Do you even care about this dilemma?" He paused as though he were expecting the dog to answer. "I can't keep finding dead people with you every time we leave this house, man." Jonas heaved a long sigh as Cairo rested his heavy head on his thigh. "Okay, I get it." He pulled his cell phone from his pocket and finally returned the call from Jana at the Allegheny Mountain Rescue Group to discuss training with Cairo.

8

"Ayy, why's Cap's doors and blinds all closed up?" Burgess inquired as he entered the squad room.

"No clue," Rainer replied.

"We got here around the same time, and they were already shut," Torrey replied. "Maybe an interview?"

"Hmmm... Good! My ol' lady is trippin' about all this overtime I've been putting in. She's just missin' Sweet Daddy," he boasted, jokingly stroking his broad chest.

Rainer and Torrey looked at each other before Torrey said to Burgess, "Man, if you ever call yourself 'Sweet Daddy' and touch your nips again in my presence, I will-"

Burgess immediately busted out laughing.

"Besides, you can't call her your ol' lady until you marry her."

"I'm thinking about it," he nodded. "*Thinking...*"

Jonas smiled nostalgically, reminiscing about his proposal to Brenna in the helicopter. "Just make it special."

"Speaking of special, did you guys see the news last night?" Rainer asked. "The guy found murdered in the park in Beaver County?"

"Yo, how the hell is that special?" Torrey asked.

"I mean... You know like special as in sick."

"Those words are not synonymous!" Burgess quipped.

"Not at all! We're gonna get you a thesaurus," Torrey laughed. "But yeah. Wanna know the craziest part? Me and Cairo walked right past there. And he wouldn't move. He knew that body was there."

"Why didn't you say something?" Rainer asked.

"Cuz I didn't know! We were jogging. I just thought he was tired. *I was*!"

It was Rainer's and Burgess' turn to exchange looks.

"I *knowww*... I know. I'm getting training so I can work with him."

"Why is Cap's door all closed up?" Ruby questioned, setting her things on the desk.

"We all asked the same thing," Rainer replied. "The only highlight you missed was Burgess seductively caressing his nips for Torrey."

"I wouldn't say I *missed* it," Ruby replied dryly, arching a carefully shaped eyebrow at the still impishly grinning Burgess.

Just as Ruby finally took a seat, the door swung open and the team waited on pins and needles to see if a potential candidate would exit the office because they were really hurting staff-wise.

Like a slow-motion scene from a movie, Penelope emerged, carrying the box of Lainey's belongings from her desk.

The sad smile on her face instantly transformed into a glare of fury and hatred when she locked eyes with Claudia from across the room. What seemed to anger Penelope most was the fact that Claudia was seated at her desk so nonchalantly - legs crossed, so relaxed, like nothing had ever happened. On a scale of 1-10, her resting bitch face was on eleven, and she seemed so unconcerned with seeing the family of the woman she had shot dead. There was no remorse on her face or in her body language, but why would there be? Ruby was quite fine with everything that had transpired.

Penelope carelessly dropped the cardboard box onto the closest desk and began to storm over toward Claudia but was intercepted by Torrey.

He stepped in front of her and spoke in a hushed tone, periodically glancing back at Claudia.

"But how can you *work* with her!?" Penelope yelled, tears beginning to form in her eyes again. "She killed your fiancée too! How is she even still *here!?*"

Ruby watched the scene unfold, taking in her perfect pale skin, now flushed from rage - the same skin she threatened to peel from Penelope's body and send to Lainey in a pretty pink box. *You already lost your fiancée. I would hate for you to have to lose your dog as well.*

Ruby could feel the smirk forming on her lips and in her eyes, so she immediately corrected it as she watched Torrey continue to quietly console her.

Ruby could also feel Denise's eyes on her from the side as she watched Torrey wrap his arm around the grieving woman to escort her through the squad room and out the double doors toward the elevator.

Shifting her eyes to her new partner, Denise seemed concerned. "You good?" Ruby asked.

"Uhhh, yeah," she nodded.

"Good."

Penelope completely broke down at the elevator, so Torrey carried the box to her car.

"I just don't understand how you can be in the same room with that monster," she cried. "Did you see her *face!?* It's like she doesn't even care!"

Torrey nodded, unsure how to respond because on the one hand, he didn't think Lainey could possibly do something like that, but on the other, if she did, Claudia would be justified in defending herself. He also couldn't stop replaying in his mind what she'd said about Lainey standing over Brenna. If she really did finish what the gunshot started.

"I just want the truth to somehow come out!" she cried.

"Yeah, same." He paused. "Hey, can you meet me tonight?" he asked, loading the box into her vehicle. "Like 7ish?"

Penelope sniffed and nodded, "Where?"

9

Penelope slowly entered and scanned the bar until she saw Jonas stand and wave her over. They hugged and took a seat just as the server came over to take their drink orders.

"I was *supposed* to be dieting to fit into a wedding gown, but since *his* colleague murdered my fiancée, I think I'll have the cheese fries and a beer. Whatever's on tap," she requested with angry sarcasm in her voice. "Please," she added.

The server's alarmed gaze drifted between the two of them because that was the last thing she expected to hear that evening. She was young and unsure of what to say so all that came out was, "And for you, sir?"

"Well, since that same colleague killed *my* fiancée as well, I'll have the same, except I'll have a Coors Light."

The server kept staring at them quietly, but no one was smiling, so she finally did, then looked around the room and asked, "Is this some hidden camera show?"

Realizing that no one was smiling and there were no cameras, she collected their menus and quickly departed the table.

"You're kind of sick, you know that, right?" Jonas chuckled.

"Hello, pot? This is kettle. You're just as bad. But did you see her face? That definitely would have made Lainey laugh."

"Yeah, Bren too."

"So why are we here?"

"Well, I heard and felt everything you were saying at the precinct. But Claudia told me something the other day and..." He paused while the server delivered the drinks.

"She said that when Lainey fired, her gun accidentally went off, hitting Brenna, but... that... Brenna was still alive after she was hit." After a few moments and a large gulp of beer, Jonas continued. "She uh... she said, without expressly saying, that she believed Lainey was the one who actually killed her."

Penelope remained calm and shook her head because watching her cocker spaniel sprout wings and take flight was more possible than Lainey intentionally killing Brenna.

"You have to know she's lying right? Lane *loved* Brenna. And Cairo! She talked about that dog like he was her own. But my question is, why?"

"She claimed that Brenna came down the hill and witnessed Lainey shoot her, so to tie up loose ends, she suggested Brenna had to go as well."

Two tears quickly rolled down Penelope's round face. "So, you believe that?"

"I honestly don't know what to believe. Do I think it's in Lainey's nature to do something that vile? Absolutely not.

But I just keep going back and forth trying to figure out how to *prove* it. Every one of us could say that she's innocent, but it's what you can prove that's important here. And no one is going to move or do anything until there's proof - like tangible irrefutable proof that Lainey could not have possibly done any of this."

Penelope exhaled, relieved.

"I'm stopping by to see the medical examiner tomorrow about one of our victims and… I'm gonna ask about Brenna."

"You sure you're ready for all that?"

"No. But I need to know the truth. That crafty bitch is out here living her best life and all in the love that we no longer have," he hissed bitterly.

Jonas sipped his beer while confessing to Penelope about his most recent visit to Costco. He'd heard a familiar laugh and when he swung around the corner, he noticed Claudia and Maceo giggling as he fed her food from one of the ladies passing out samples. His heart felt sick watching them together, seeing how fond of her Maceo was - observing how they looked at one another… how gentle and nurturing he was with her. He had that once and Claudia took it from him. Jonas' body temperature elevated as his heart rate increased, staring at the two of them with narrowed, hateful eyes. But curiosity replaced the rage when he noticed a man at the other side of the store who appeared to be watching the couple as well.

He squinted to try to clear his vision because the person resembled the FBI agent but was nowhere near as clean-cut and well-put together. Weston didn't notice Jonas, because he seemed so focused on what Claudia and Maceo were doing.

"He didn't look well."

"Are you sure it was him?" she asked.

"I mean, I *feel* like it was, but this guy was kinda jacked," he said, flexing his much leaner muscles. "So if it *was* him, he been hittin' the weights - *hard*. Have you seen him since Alessandra's accident?"

"I went to visit him and the boys once afterward... before Lainey... but I haven't seen him since her service. I would have thought he'd be back to work by now."

"Not looking like that."

"Hmmm... Okay, then what happened?"

"Nothing. I watched him watching her, which is admittedly kinda creepy.

"Definitely," she agreed. "Do you think it was because he suspects she had something to do with Alessandra's accident?"

"Not sure. But you and I both know she didn't because she was still at the party."

"Was she?"

"Well, I know Maceo was."

"But they didn't come together. They all drove separately. I remember Claudia telling Lainey about her new Telluride outside."

"She's always been pretty anal about her vehicles, I can't envision her crashing her brand new one into anyone, honestly. Also, hitting another vehicle at such a high rate of speed, I would think both airbags would have deployed, which means the driver would have sustained some sort of facial injuries. I saw Claudia the very next day, and her face was fine."

"So it really could have been just a genuine car accident?"

"Oh no, someone absolutely hit her car. The way the back end was dented was not consistent with her just spinning out and flipping on a wet road. Plus, there was paint transfer. The techs lifted it and, according to Lainey, they matched it to a black Mercedes."

"How is that going to help when there are thousands of them?"

"There are. But given the tire marks on the road and the height of the transfer marks, they could tell it was a larger model vehicle. It would have sustained hella damage so they would just start with the local body shops and see if anyone worked on that brand and what was repaired."

Penelope nodded, and they sat in silence for a few moments.

"So. Between us, I kind of took something from Lainey's desk. Her notepad. She was always jotting stuff down in that thing, and she drew something that I wanted to run past you… see if maybe you knew what it was or what it meant?"

"Sure."

He flipped through until he came to the page with the drawing.

"What is it? What are these squiggles?" she asked.

"Damn. I was hoping you could tell me."

She stared at it a little longer. "Sorry, I got nothing. So where do we go from here?"

"I'm not sure, but we're not leaving this bar until we figure out a plan, a way, a method, *something* to find additional evidence that clears Lainey's name and proves that Claudia is lying."

"Well, our server is *not* going to like that," she chuckled.

A cold darkness clouded his eyes. "I'm a detective with just as much criminalistics knowledge as this Keeper. You were engaged to one of us, so I *know* you picked up some knowledge. Plus, you're a photographer slick with Photoshop. If the Keeper can abduct and murder people and not get caught, so can we."

"Jonas!" Penelope gasped. "Murder though? I- You're not serious… right?" she leaned closer to whisper. "Can't you just take her and like, break some fingers or something until she comes clean?"

He stared at his adorably innocent friend pensively then thought, *I'd rather just slowly kill her and set the house on fire.*

10

"How'd it go?" Captain Higgins asked Burgess and Rainer.

"Not so hot," Burgess answered warily. "We canvassed the neighborhood, spoke to residents, checked the video cam footage of those who had it available. No footage of anyone on foot."

"And of the people who did have cameras, many of them didn't extend to the street to get a full image of any cars," Rainer added. "Because if so, that would have their doorbells triggering all the time unnecessarily."

"There was one security camera about six houses down that had access to the one-way street, but only two cars drove past in the vicinity of the time of death. The resident recognized his neighbor's vehicles, so the cars were likely just driving home."

"So if the killer isn't one of the neighbors, then the person maybe parked elsewhere and came down through the back?" Rainer questioned.

"Mmm! That must be it. The next-door neighbor was still up and her motion sensor light went off in the back of her house, she said. But when she got up to look out, she didn't see anything. She just assumed it was some local wildlife."

The captain loudly exhaled. "This is not helpful at all."

"Sorry, Cap."

"What about the husband?"

"Spoke to him too. They don't live together. Separated. But none of that mattered because he had an alibi," Rainer replied.

"And you verified it?"

"Sure did," Burgess answered. "That's what took us so long to get back. He was actually with a young lady at the Steelers game - showed us his ticket stubs. Her T.O.D. was around the time the game ended, but Heinz Field's CCTV-"

"You mean Acrisure," Rainer interrupted.

Both men looked at her frowning, knowing that *they* could call it whatever they wanted but that was still Heinz Field. Hell, to the captain, it was still Three Rivers Stadium.

"Sure... Acri-whatever..." Burgess snipped. "Either way, that man has a solid alibi."

"Honestly, that's like the perfect time to skulk about the suburbs. Like eighty percent of Pittsburgh is posted up in front of their televisions with the volume up, screaming and cheering. Who's paying attention to anything else? Especially when they were playing in overtime within their division?"

"Why do you keep saying *they* and *their*? You're not a Steelers fan?"

"Burgess. I'm from Baltimore, baby," she replied with proud sass.

"Look, I'm not trying to tell anyone how to do their jobs here. But you can fire her now, Cap," he said, shaking his head. "How is this not part of the standard interview questionnaire?"

Higgins rolled his eyes. "Where are Torrey and Martinez?" he questioned, looking toward the elevator.

"Oh, they swung by the M.E.'s office to see if there are any updates on the victim."

"Together? They went *together*?" he nervously asked.

They nodded.

"Ooookayyy... Maybe this is a good thing."

The ride over to the medical examiner's office was tense and quiet. In the passenger seat, Ruby could feel the rage and resentment that emanated from Torrey. As annoying as it sometimes was, she had gotten used to rides where Lainey literally didn't shut up. She always had so much to say about everything, so sitting in silence with a person who hated her was slightly awkward.

Torrey on the other hand, was driving on autopilot while thinking about the case... And the fact that he felt a little weird being alone with the person he had been covertly watching. Someone he once trusted was now someone he wouldn't even spit on if she were on fire. Probably not the best attitude in their dangerous line of work. But something about her story, he just didn't... believe.

As they approached the busy intersection, his eyes shifted to Claudia as his thoughts went to flooring it, jumping out, and leaving the car to speed through the red light, causing a horrific accident. But that would injure or kill more people than just her, and he didn't want anyone else to feel the type of pain that he was going through. So, instead, he slammed on the brakes at the last second, causing them both to lurch forward as the car came to an abrupt halt.

"Sorry," he offered dryly.

"Kaaath!" Torrey exclaimed, happily announcing their presence. He sounded completely different from the bitter man in the car a few minutes prior.

Dr. Kathryn Hale's gray eyes lit up when she smiled to greet the detectives.

"Jonas! Claudia! Hello!" she said, rising from behind her desk. You must be here about Kelly Knight?"

"We are," Ruby answered.

"Working on that report now, but the drug in question was heroin. It was made to look like an overdose."

"So she *was* actually left-handed?" Torrey asked.

"Based on the differences in musculature between the two arms, yes, it is safe to say she was left-handed."

"Then whoever killed her had to have known of her history of drug use. I mean, she was pretty young at the time and looked to have been clean for decades, but history is history I guess?" Torrey assessed.

"Exactly, because when police came in to assess the scene, they would have ruled it a suicide and been done. You guys were called in only because I noticed her watch. Had she been someone who didn't wear one at all, it's doubtful that an autopsy would have even been performed."

Ruby held her breath the entire time Kathryn spoke and had to remind herself to breathe. A fucking timepiece had her discussing a woman whose death should have immediately been ruled an overdose and should never have involved her squad.

"There wasn't much in her stomach other than a bit of tequila. It was such a small amount, in fact, that if I were a betting woman, I would say she didn't drink this of her own volition."

Ruby's heart rate began to hasten.

"You mean like whoever injected her then forced the drink into her?"

"Yes. Or else she somehow completely missed her mouth," she remarked sarcastically. "I found traces of the tequila on her chin, neck, down the sides of her face, and in her hair as though she aspirated while it was being forced in while she was lying down."

Breathe.

Ruby inhaled. "That's horrible," she uttered, still breathing deeply, subtly massaging her tingling left arm.

Torrey stared at Claudia but directed his question to Kathryn. "Hey uhhh, while I'm here, I'd like to ask you a question about my fiancée, Brenna Barlowe."

Ruby swiftly raised her lowered eyes to meet his, then averted them to await a response from the M.E.

"Sure, Jonas. I'll answer what I can," she replied, feeling the palpable tension mount between the two detectives.

"Was it *really* the gunshot wound that killed her? Or could there have possibly been some other... cause of death?"

Ruby's heart continued to thud heavily in her chest. This was why he wanted her to join him here.

Stay cool. He's just trying to get a rise out of you and see how you'll respond to this line of questioning.

"Um... I'm not sure what you mean."

"It's been... *suggested* that the bullet took her down, but she might have... died in another manner," he stated, returning his gaze to Kathryn.

"Such as?"

"Uh, suffocation," Torrey replied emotionally.

"You're asking if she could have possibly still been alive after the gunshot wound but subsequently suffocated?"

Breathe, Ruby.

He nodded.

"Jonas, an autopsy was not performed. And based on the alignment of everyone's statements, neither the county nor the department requested one. The family didn't either. But uh... a death of that nature might involve some postmortem bruising to the face. However, because of Brenna's darker skin tone, it makes it more difficult to see with the naked eye. With that information earlier, I would have been able to use a special light to enable the detection of bruising on more melanated skin surfaces.

"But with that being said, if that were to have happened after a gunshot wound, with her bleeding out, the person who allegedly would have closed her nose and mouth would not have had to apply much pressure. Thus, there may not have been any bruising present at all."

Kathryn noted Jonas' sunken eyes and pained facial expression. "Do you want me to stop?"

He shook his head no.

Keep. Breathing.

Kathryn swallowed before continuing. "Typically, in victims of asphyxiation, we see petechiae... Uhh, when the tiny blood vessels rupture in soft tissues such as the whites of the eyes."

"Did she have that?" he asked hurriedly.

"She did, but again, since petechiae can occur anytime oxygen and blood flow are cut off and blood pressure increases and no official autopsy was conducted, I attributed it to the gunshot wound. Additionally, after death, petechiae occurs in the eyes when the body has lain face up for a length of time.

"So, *could* she have been asphyxiated after the gunshot wound? It is possible. But not having that information at her time of death, and with no autopsy, her cause of death was listed as exsanguination due to a gunshot wound to the upper chest."

Exhale.

"I need a minute," Torrey huffed, storming out of the office.

The two ladies stood together in silence for a few moments. "I'm sorry. Thank you for the information, Kathryn."

"You're welcome. This... must be difficult - working together like this?"

"It is. And I feel terrible about what happened," she lied.

HIDDEN DARKNESS

11

Okay... I'm here. And Claudia is not. She hasn't been for a while, so I'm positive there's no way that Ring doorbell still has battery life. But just in case, I decide to approach like a visitor.

It's dead. Perfect.

I try the front door just in case, but not surprisingly, it's locked. With my trusty black bag of essentials, I swing around to the back. Locked. I head down around to the basement door, which looks newer than the others. Also locked. But of course, I know how to pick them. My eyes wander up the steps to her deck with the sliding door. What are the odds that it got locked when Maceo claimed in his statement to have run out to find her that night?

As the setting sun casts ominous shadows across the yard from the nearby trees, I sneak up the steps and give the sliding glass a push, and it unexpectedly opens! This means her alarm is not set, otherwise it would have gone off. I know she deactivated the cameras after she killed Tanner because she is not a fan of being surveilled.

I enter and observe her clean, trendy home, with a new African canvas painting, barely out of the packaging, taking up much of the dining room table. Setting my bag down on the massive kitchen island, I pull out the borrowed metal detection wand and begin to scan that area first. It beeps when we come to the drawers, so I open the first one to find silverware, then the second to find potholders. I shift them around and there is a gun. Nice.

Next, I move to the dining room, where I find one affixed to the underside of the table, and then to the living room where I find one under the end table and another in the potted artificial plant by the fireplace.

I have four guns so far and I haven't even made it out of the main living space yet. What the hell is wrong with this woman?

There are no guns in any of the guest rooms but I do, however, find three very well-hidden sharp knives and pepper gel, so I add them to the growing pile of weapons.

Continuing to scan, I locate the gun in the master bathroom cupboard, and, to my surprise, one under her pillow. Why would this not be in the nightstand? Makes sense why loved ones aren't safe around her - this bitch literally goes to bed with murder on her mind. How has she not accidentally shot herself... or anyone else in this bed with her?

I stare down at this large pile of weaponry, wondering what war this woman is all ready to single-handedly fight. Then I consider the fact that I did just break into her home, so there's that. And I guess the last detective who came to her home attacked her, so... never mind.

With my already gloved hands, I load her six firearms, four pepper sprays, and three knives into my bag. I also relocate the holder full of eight cutting knives to the cabinet above her refrigerator and remove all of the sharp knives from the silverware drawer in addition to the scissors.

I then remove the small burgundy case containing twelve miniature motion sensor cameras and hide them strategically throughout her home after linking them all to my phone's app, even though there's nothing to see here... yet.

I throw the bag over my shoulder, unlock a guest room window, and then exit through the still-unlocked sliding glass door.

12

Ruby quietly climbed back into bed beside Maceo, who had turned in early, wondering why he had been so exhausted some nights.

He was sound asleep, but electricity was coursing through Ruby's body after what she'd just pulled off. It was beautiful. Dan Hogan was the latest target checked off her little hit list. He was the pervert who snuck in under the radar. Parents warn their children about these people every day, but he was kind with genuine eyes and a love for the arts. He was teaching them how to play the piano in a home with his wife and two children. How much of a threat could he be, right?

Ruby thought back to the story his wife told of silently standing at the entryway to his music room, watching her husband on his knees behind the piano bench, using one hand to guide his 8-year-old student's fingers on the keys. The fingertips of his other hand, however, were lightly gliding up and down her lower back.

This was a preemptive strike. His wife didn't know if he had done anything worse than that yet, but the way he jumped up and away from the child when she cleared her throat to announce her presence was enough for her to nip all of it in the bud. She had two young daughters from a previous relationship and there was no way she could overlook that billboard-sized red flag.

Ruby's core began to throb with excitement when she thought back about using her dashboard emergency lights to pull *Disgusting Dan* over on the desolate road. One thing about Pittsburgh is the number of roads without overhead streetlights vastly outnumbered the illuminated streets.

His guard instantly lowered when he saw that she was a woman because, of course, a woman wasn't capable of hurting a big strapping man. Sure… Okay…

She flashed her badge, requested his license and registration, and asked him to please step out of the vehicle.

She began to touch herself, becoming even more physically aroused at the thought of him shifting to unbuckle his seatbelt, unaware of the gun pointed at him. She put a bullet in his chest and the second in his head, point blank.

With her gloved hands, she put the registration back in his glove box but rifled through it and the center console, leaving the center lid up. After retrieving the shell casings from the bullets, she put his license back in the wallet that she stuffed into her pocket and then removed the two rings and the watch he was wearing. She turned off the car and left the passenger door open to make it look like someone else had been in the car with him. Whoever that was, maybe *they* robbed and shot him?

Now for the rest of her alibi...

Ruby looked over at Mace, still peacefully sleeping. She pulled the covers down, exposing his taut nude body, how he also preferred to sleep, just like her. Taking him into her warm, wet mouth, he began to unconsciously stiffen and rouse slightly, even though he was still hazy from the drugs she had slipped him at dinner.

In a slight fog, still not completely awake, he mumbled, "Baby what are you- ahhhh..." he moaned.

"Shhhh..." she ordered, continuing to service him until he was fully erect, and she was able to climb on top to have her way with him.

"Ohhh gahhh..." he uttered as she slid him inside her aching center.

As she began to smoothly glide her body up and down, she kissed him. "I just needed you so bad... Right now... I just needed to feel you... inside," she groaned into his mouth between kisses.

Was he fully conscious? No. Was he functional enough to recall waking up to her mouth wrapped around him? More than likely.

They both moaned in ecstasy as she took his body without his consent, all to solidify an alibi just in case. At that moment, *she* was technically the sexual predator. But it was okay in her mind because had he not been drugged by her, he would have absolutely been down to forcefully fuck her until her hair straightened on its own.

Both of their orgasms were so intense that she fell asleep right there on top with him still inside of her.

Maceo awakened startled by a feeling of being weighed down until he realized that it was just his sexy-ass girl on top of him. As he continued shifting, she awakened as well, groggy but with a smile. "What did you do to me last night?" she questioned flirtatiously.

"Excuse me? I went to bed early. And yo, you're on top of *me*! You rolled over and just stole my virtue in the night," he said jokingly, covering his nipples with his hands.

"Your virtue? *Okay...*" she laughed, getting up from the bed. "Glad you remember. I'm hopping in the shower."

"Oooh, me too," he exclaimed, jumping out of bed. "I need to wash your... everything."

13

Torrey pulled up to the Allegheny Mountain Rescue Group headquarters with Cairo. The thick fog hanging heavily in the air barely allowed the autumn sun's rays to break through.

"Mornin' Detective! Hellooo Cai!"

Jonas greeted the director, Jana, as Cairo sprinted over to the kind woman he immediately recognized. She opened her door to release her pup, who adored the affectionate Doberman.

"So glad you finally made it out to us."

"Yeah... Had I known what I was looking for, the guy in the park could have been located two days earlier. We were right there."

"Ohhh... He sat down for ya, huh?"

"Yes! He wouldn't move! I thought he was just tired."

Jana laughed, "He's in better shape than *both* of us! No, he was waiting for you to let him know what a good boy he was for finding what you were looking for."

"Trust me. I was *not* looking for that!"

Jana laughed, "We never are. But they always are. They're pretty special," she admired, watching the two sturdy canines sniff around the grassy outdoor area together.

"I could have sworn Brenna told me at some point that he lays down or something."

"Some dogs do, but Cairo's end command is to sit. He'll only lie down if he's already sitting, like when he's on the water. My pittie, Mia, will whimper before she lies down when we're boating."

"Oh, yours does water detection as well? I didn't know this was such a common thing."

"It's not. Of course, they can smell it, but just like anything else we want to excel in, training and practice need to happen. When Brenna mentioned how much she loved being in and on the water, I told her about how I trained my Mia girl, and she was up for the task... Now we have Cairo," she smiled.

The pair spent the next hour and a half working with Jana and Mia, learning the different commands and protocols for when they arrive at a search location. Since Jonas was a detective and already familiar with crime scenes, she was able to speed through much of that information. He also learned about how the decomposition of remains affects the soil, which enables the dogs to locate the victims. Jonas would need to spend more time in the field working with Cairo, but they were at least off to a good start. He felt confident knowing he was leaving with some helpful knowledge about his dog's skill set.

"Hey," he turned back to Jana as they were leaving. "One more question."

Digging in his back pocket for Lainey's small notepad, he opened it and flipped through the pages until he got to the drawing. "You don't by chance know what this means? It's on a page where my colleague had some notes about cadaver dogs. I thought maybe the two of them were somehow connected?"

Jana squinted, staring at the strange diagram. "No... Hmmm..." she said, still examining it. "The only thing I could think of is possibly a rough drawing of a search location? But I'm not sure what this giant "V" is for," she said, still scrutinizing it.

"Yeah, same. I thought maybe an arrow pointing down? But I'm not sure to what because there's nothing on the next page except more writing."

"Sorry I couldn't be more help."

"No, this was all very helpful. Thank you."

He opened the door for Cairo to hop in, then turned around once more. "Oh hey! One more question," he laughed. "I'm sorry, for real this time."

"It's fine." She laughed as well.

"Can he smell the uh, the... *death* on people?"

"I imagine he could, depending on how recent and close the interactions were."

"Hmmm... Okay, thanks again," Jonas murmured distractedly, hopping into his car, wondering if that's why Cairo sat at Martinez's desk.

14

Ruby strolled over to answer the knock at the door after being granted access by security. Of course, it was Claudia's sister Hope bringing food, even though she was well enough to fend for herself in that area. As weird as she found this woman, she had to admit she could really throw down in the kitchen.

"Hey sweetness!" Hope gushed as she assaulted her sister with a warm embrace. Ruby was starting to get used to these attacks. She didn't like them, but she knew they were going to happen regardless. "Where are your clothes, baby?"

"In the drawer where they belong," Ruby said, sashaying through the kitchen in only a pair of red boy shorts and a cut-off tee.

Rolling her eyes, Hope began to unload meal prep for two. "Well, here is your deer. I cooked you a damn *deer*... And all the other proteins you requested."

"Thanks," Ruby said, inspecting the container of food. "It smells great. Are you going to let me pay you for this?"

"Nope. You're my sister. I love taking care of you, and I love cooking," she stated, continuing to unload the bag. "So how has it been crashing here with that sexy ass man? Must be why you don't wear clothes anymore."

"Shhh... He's still here."

"I do not care! That man *knows* I think he's fine. I can look as long as I'm not touching."

I would break every one of your fingers if you touched him. "Hmmm... So yeah, it's been interesting. I'm not used to having someone around all the time and being constantly monitored. I enjoy my freedom, but I also enjoy his company, as weird as that is."

"That's not weird, CoCo. It's normal," Hope laughed. "I see how you get all girly when you talk about him."

Girly? Ewww. I better work on fixing that.

"Have you been back home at all?"

"Not yet."

"Well, you really should get back out there if for nothing more than to make sure everything is okay and locked up and whatnot."

"You're probably right. Honestly, I just haven't felt like driving all that way."

"Well, welcome to *my* world, ma'am! Maybe you will consider selling the house and staying here with your boo thang. That way, we don't have to drive so far to see you."

Ruby plastered a fake smile across her face as she thought, *other than you dropping off this delicious food, I would be fine with never actually seeing you again.*

"So, whatever happened with-"

"Ayyy sis!" Maceo exclaimed as he exited their bedroom.

"Oh, I'm sis now?"

"Damn right," he said, giving her the type of hug that she always tried to give her sister. "As soon as I marry that *foine* ass woman over there," he said, grinning at Ruby.

"Marriage?" *Who said anything about marriage?* She thought, scrutinizing the two of them.

"When you know, you know," Maceo said, lifting her chin and planting a soft kiss on her lips, then smacking the side of her cheek that the boy shorts left exposed.

With a goofy smile, Hope watched her sister and this man, who appeared to make her so happy. She was pleased that Claudia would get to experience what she and her husband have.

Meanwhile, Ruby was trying to figure out how any of this happened. She literally just came for the sex, and now she was basically living with this man.

"This is a lotta food," Mace observed.

"Half of that she brought for you."

"Awww, that's what's up! Thanks! It looks so good! I'mma dig in as soon as I get back," he said, grabbing his holstered firearm.

"Where you going?"

"Got a call from the director. Gotta head out. Probably gonna be a late one - we're still short with Weston not back from his leave yet. But I'll check in." He smiled before planting three more kisses on Ruby's lips, cheek, and neck. Walking toward the door, he held her hand until the distance separated them.

Why the fuck is she looking at me like that?

"You guys are so stinkin' adorable!" Hope announced.

Ruby could feel her face begin to contort in disgust, but quickly fixed it to stare at her blankly, unsure of how to respond to that horrific observation. Not one part of her life's objective was to be seen as adorable.

"So, speaking of Weston, what happened with you two? You guys were pretty cute together too, even though he was married and you guys... really *shouldn't* have been that cute," she rambled. "After his wife left the picture, I figured you two would be doing your thing, then you show up with this hot chocolate."

"Yeah... Ummm... we just decided we would be better apart," Ruby replied, leaning over the kitchen island like she often did.

"Well, this works out because now you don't have to play stepmother to grieving children who will forever compare you to their real mama."

"Facts."

"Okay so, I gotta run. Picking up the boys from their grandma's house. She asked to keep them overnight and take them to the Children's Museum and I was like, yes, please! Thank you!"

"Ohhh, so you and hubby got to get it crackin' last night huh?"

"Girl! *Everywhere!* That shit needs to happen more often."

Hope hugged Ruby and then headed out.

Ruby looked at her Apple watch as she removed it, deciding that with Maceo gone for the night, it would be an excellent opportunity to go hunting and finish up the third person on her list.

Jonas pulled out his phone to respond to a call from Penelope.

"Did you receive the photos I sent?"

"I did. They're good – very helpful," he replied, the two of them speaking vaguely. She was a photographer after all, so there was nothing suspicious about this conversation if it were to ever come to light. He needed photos taken; she took them. Did it matter that the images he needed were of Claudia? Yes, but no one ever needed to know that.

"So, you're good to go on your end?"

"I am. I'll keep you posted but from the other phone."

"Okay."

15

He quietly watched from the shadows, out of camera range, as Claudia sat in her vehicle. She wasn't in her new Telluride. Turns out, she kept her Toyota RAV4 instead of trading it in.

She eventually exited the car and slowly made her way across the garage when the dark figure barely emerged from the shadows.

Startled, she squinted and asked, "What are you *doing* here? Are you *following* me?"

"I am. And I saw everything," he said, waving his phone.

With narrowed eyes, she replied, "Liar."

"*Am* I, though? I watched you follow that man, illegally pull him over in a civilian vehicle, then murder him in cold blood."

Fuck. "What do you want?"

"You… to come with me."

Ruby glared at him as she slowly reached for her hip.

"Uh, uh, uhhh…" he threatened, aiming the gun with a silencer that looked eerily similar to hers. "Don't even *think* about it. Come," he ordered.

With her heart racing, she hesitantly made her way toward the gunman, chastising herself for not realizing she was being tailed. He must have had his lights out. She contemplated how she could get out of this situation. Under normal circumstances, she would choose fight over flight. However, with her arm currently compromised, she knew she could never effectively overpower him. But she had to *try*. You fight and die where you stand before allowing your captor to transport you to a secondary location, where only worse things await.

As she approached him, with intimidation in her gaze, Ruby worked diligently to display confidence, but inside, her stomach churned. Her math skills may not have been so accurate when it came to drugging the predators she planned to kill anyway, but everything about her computer skills was on point. She knew damn well there was no camera coverage in the garage right now and on four of the floors of the building. Could they have located and fixed the "glitch" by now? It was possible, but unlikely. But even still, she knew he was in an area not covered by the camera if it were working. He wasn't stupid.

She stared at him, dismissively looked him up and down, and boldly declared, "There are cameras everywhere. You're not going to hurt me."

"No. You're right," he whispered, roughly snatching her toward him, digging his thumb into the wounded part of her shoulder which halted her from reaching again for her gun. "I'm not gonna *just* hurt you. I'm gonna *kill* you," he whispered.

She huffed and winced as the pain shot through her chest and down her arm, and her knees slightly weakened. She wasn't going to scream or cry out to give him the satisfaction of knowing just *how* much he had hurt her.

Ruby's fist made contact with his face but fueled with rage, he hardly noticed. He struck her across the face, sending her painfully to the ground. With anger and disgust coursing through him, he pressed his foot into her injured shoulder, finally forcing her to cry out. He reached down to remove her gun from its secured holster, then forcefully jabbed a sharp syringe into her inner thigh while she aggressively scratched and clawed at him.

As the room began to spin and the walls felt like they were closing in around her, Ruby gasped for breath. Her vision blurred and her entire body involuntarily relaxed as she felt his large hands roaming it to check for other weapons. She didn't have any. There was no need to bring anything extra and risk dropping or losing it.

She wasn't unconscious, but she wasn't lucid either. Everything was hazy as he snatched her up from the ground, leaned her weight onto him, and slowly guided her out of the back exit where there was camera coverage, but it was sparse.

"Whyy are…" Her voice trailed off.

He knew where to go and how to move to be detected the least. He turned down the alley and injected her once more, causing her to fully pass out. After loading her into the trunk of his waiting car, he sat there for a little while before driving through the city's alleys and side roads to make his way to their final destination.

"Baybeee!" Maceo called out, returning home. The only reason he did so at that late hour was because the lights and television were still on, thus he naturally assumed she was there, waiting up for him. "Man, wait till you hear about this shit! And I am *starvin'*! I can't wait to get into some of Hope's food!" he said, removing his shoes, hanging up his jacket, and dropping his remaining belongings onto the kitchen island.

Still receiving no response, he peeked into the living room. "Baby?"

He scanned the large open space and then made his way to the bedroom. "Rubes? You in here, babe?"

His eyes made their way across the pristine room, then to the en suite bathroom, which was dark. His stomach twisted and nerves began to take over, thinking about where she could be and if she was okay. It wasn't like her to just vanish. Then he thought about how not too long ago the mayor of the damn city paid him to kill her. What if she'd found someone else? Maceo ran to his phone on the island and began to frantically call her.

"Come on... Pick up, pick up, pick up," he mumbled as the phone rang several times before going to voicemail. So, at least he knew it was still on and could be tracked, if necessary. He tried once more, but as it rang this time, he heard a loud thud from the master bedroom. Still allowing it to ring, he retrieved his gun from atop the island and made his way back to the source of the noise.

As the call again went to voicemail, Mace hung up and redialed, slowly continuing to the bedroom. He exhaled and shoved his gun into the back of his pants when he realized that her cell, still attached to the charger, had vibrated off of the nightstand and onto the floor. His heart began to race with anxiety because she wouldn't just leave her phone.

He immediately called Hope, who after three attempts, finally groggily answered.

"Hey, I'm so sorry to wake you, but have you seen or heard from Ru- uh, Claudia?" he asked with urgency in his voice. He'd gotten so used to calling her Ruby that it instinctively almost slipped out.

"What? Not since I left your place earlier. She's not there?"

"I came back, the lights were still on but she's not here. Her phone is, though."

That caused Hope to instantly sit up in bed and wake her husband. "Okay, um... what about her car? Is it still there?"

"I don't know. I'll run down now and check. I'll call you back," he said briskly, hanging up and darting out of the apartment.

When Maceo came upon Ruby's shiny, black SUV in its usual spot, he slowly approached and pulled the handle to see if it was unlocked. It wasn't.

"Shit!"

He ran back in and hastily questioned the security team in the front lobby, then immediately called to wake Captain Higgins.

16

A prickly sensation covered Ruby's entire body as she began to come to. Still very hazy, she felt like her eyes were open, but blackness still surrounded her. She swallowed slowly, but everything was so dry, she could feel the tightness in and around her mouth.

"Hello?" She tried to speak, but in her weakened state, it barely came out.

Breathing deeply in through her nose, Ruby struggled for the air that she felt like she'd been deprived of after being drugged. Then it made her wonder if this was how Maceo felt after she had drugged *him*.

Straining to see through the darkness, her eyes were still heavy, and her head was still foggy, but the room had a familiar smell. Actually, there were a *few* familiar scents intermingling once she thought about it. It's been said that when one sense is removed, the others are heightened, but she never realized how much until that moment.

There was nothing to be heard. Silence surrounded her aching body while she listened intently for any noise that would indicate where she was being held.

"Hello?" Ruby managed to groan a little louder that time.

Still silence.

She moaned as the rumbling of her stomach exacerbated the hunger pains. Why hadn't she eaten the food that Hope delivered before leaving that night? Ruby struggled to figure out the last time she had anything to eat. *Breakfast. And that was only egg whites and turkey sausage.*

How long had she even been out? The room was black. Was that because it was still night? Or was it daytime, and she was being held underground? But why would anywhere underground smell familiar? Just a few of the questions that struggled to cross her mind.

As Ruby became more aware of her body, it seemed to trigger more feelings of pain. The mind was incredibly tricky like that. *Everything... hurts*, she thought to herself, still struggling to gain full lucidity. The fingers on her left hand began to involuntarily twitch as a result of the nerve damage. Pain shot down the entire arm and across her chest and upper back. It wasn't until she made an attempt to manually soothe it that she realized she was very heavily restrained to the wooden chair in which she was seated.

What the actual hell? I'm absolutely going to kill the mother fucker who did this to me. Then she struggled to even recall *who* did this to her. Had she seen his face? Was he in some sort of mask? That part was also blurry. Had he injected her with something that affected her short-term memory?

Even more infuriated with her inability to recollect something so important, she fought to try to move her lower body, since she had considerably more leg strength, but nothing.

Pulling against the taut restraint around her trim waist brought attention to the fact that her bladder was full and throbbing.

"Is anyone here?" she managed to barely utter, unaware if she was even loud enough for anyone to hear her. In her throbbing head, it sounded like she was screaming but as sore and parched as her throat was, there was no possible way she could have been. "I need water... And to use the bathroom..." she begged, listening intently for any indication that someone had heard her or was even nearby.

Still silence.

Ruby knew she could only survive so long without water. Beginning to panic a little more because she was still unable to recall who took her, didn't know how long she had been gone, and wasn't sure if they had just left her there to die, she struggled against the restraints, aggressively tugging, twisting, shaking, but to no avail. Securely attached to that chair, she rocked and shifted so violently that it caused the chair to tip over. Ruby screamed out in agony when she landed on her injured side, and her head was knocked off the hard floor. Before it rendered her completely unconscious, she felt the warmth of her bladder involuntarily release, and she was powerless to stop it.

While it may have been near pitch black where he had deposited Claudia, he watched her from his laptop with a perverse smile etched onto his face. The HD camera vividly caught her confusion turning to fear, then her struggling to escape his expertly placed restraints. It was perfection. A feeling of satisfaction swelled in his chest as he thought about completely breaking her as payback for what she had done.

17

In the elevator on the way to work, Torrey breathed heavily while speaking to Brenna's mother. Penelope beeped in, but he sent her to voicemail and continued his conversation.

"Yes, I'm doing everything I can to get more information about this."

Penelope beeped in again, and once more, he sent her to voicemail.

"I know," he said empathetically. "I'm working on some things with a... colleague and I swear we *will* uncover the truth and get justice for our girl. Did you reach out to that attorney I suggested about filing a civil suit?"

Sending Penelope to voicemail for a third time, he promised in his mind to call her back as soon as he finished with his current call.

"Ok, good. And sure, I can definitely bring Cairo by for a visit this weekend... Love you too, Mama Anita."

Ending his call, then scrolling through his log for Penelope's number, he didn't notice the extra people or feel the heightened tension in the squad room until he looked up from his phone.

"What the hell..." Torrey mumbled.

"Torrey! Great, perfect timing! Get over here!" the captain shouted.

"What's goin' on, Cap?" he asked, dropping his things onto his desk.

He approached to find the entire team and Maceo surrounding their tech guy, Tony. On his large monitor was an image of a dozen small screens that represented twelve different camera locations. He was intently scrolling through as the team invaded his personal space, searching for something.

"What do you mean what's going on? Don't you watch the news? Martinez is missing. We suspect she was taken sometime late last night," Higgins explained. The captain continued talking, but Torrey's mind drifted, and while he could see his mouth moving, nothing registered after that first sentence.

"Torrey," Higgins said, waiting for a reply. When one didn't come, "Jonas!" he boomed.

"Yeah... Ummm, that's crazy."

Hearing that oddly impartial response, Maceo turned to look at Torrey for a few moments before asking suspiciously, "Ayy man, why you breathin' all funny?"

He didn't realize that his elevated heart rate had unconsciously caused him to breathe a little quicker than normal. "Oh, just shocked and worried for Claudia. You see anything on here yet?" he asked, changing the subject and sending Penelope to voicemail once more.

"Nah. Still lookin'."

"So uhh, how'd you get this footage so fast? You didn't need a warrant for this?"

"Not when you have friends in high places. Manager gave it to me when I asked."

They watched what seemed to be all normal footage of residents coming and going until Tony sped past the timeframe Maceo would have arrived home.

"Wait! Stop!"

"What's up?" Tony asked.

"Back it up," Mace ordered.

"See! That, right there! Timestamp reads 1:56 a.m. That's around the time I came home."

"But you aren't on any of this footage," Rainer observed, noticing how ripped his arms looked beneath the fitted sweater he was wearing, but realized how inappropriate that was.

"Exactly! Cuz this ain't a live feed. Someone looped this old footage."

"Aww damn," Higgins moaned, doing his obligatory *shit I'm stressed-out* body pat in search of the cigarette he knew he was going to need very shortly. "That's high-tech. Could it be someone else the mayor hired?"

Torrey stood quietly listening to the room speculate, still trying to control his breathing.

"That's what I thought last night," Mace replied, pulling out his phone to take the incoming call. "Hey, Hope..."

"Torrey. My office," Higgins ordered.

He followed, shutting the door behind them. "What's up, Cap?"

"So uhh... Look. I'm just gonna ask you this. Where were you last night?"

"Me?"

"No, Michael Jackson," he replied sarcastically. "*Yes*, you!"

"You think *I* took her?"

"I'm just asking you a question. That's it."

"I was at home... with Cairo." As it crossed his lips, Jonas realized if he were being questioned as an actual suspect, that was the shittiest alibi ever.

"Alone?"

"Captain. The beautiful soul I was about to marry was just gunned down. Of course I was alone."

"And the person who just happened to have 'gunned down,'" he said, using air quotes, "that 'soul' is now mysteriously missing."

"I would never-" His voice trailed off.

"Look, I have to ask. You've had public confrontations with her... snarky comments... All while she was trying to genuinely apologize to you for this horrific accident."

His phone buzzed in his hand once more. "Cap I'm sorry, I really have to take this. It's like the fifth call."

Higgins nodded as Torrey quickly jogged out of the office, heading toward the elevator area for some privacy away from the rest of the squad.

As soon as the call picked up, Penelope blurted, "Jonas, I've been calling you!"

"I know, sorry, I-"

"You said you were going to keep me updated! What happened? Did you get her to tell you anything? Why didn't you let me know you have her?"

He slowly exhaled, "Because I don't."

"What!? What do you mean? It's all over the news that she's missing."

"But it wasn't *me* who took her," he whispered. "I- I wasn't able to do it yet. Then I got a little nervous and-"

"Nervous!?" Penelope yelled. "This was *your* idea! And now you're bitching up on me?"

"I wasn't *bitchin' up*, I just needed to make sure I could get it done undetected. I had devised a plan and then strolled into work to find total chaos learning that someone beat me to it. They think that the mayor may have hired someone else to take her."

"Mayor Conrad!? Why?"

"Long story. I'll explain later. I gotta run - I'll get back with you soon," he said, zipping through the glass doors to grab the keys from his desk.

As Jonas approached the expansive property, he immediately noticed the impressive home. However, the landscaping left much to be desired. It had clearly been neglected and was overgrown.

He slowly pulled into the parking circle in front of the main entrance and parked behind the red official-looking SUV.

"Are you the owner of this eyesore?" the short, slender man holding the clipboard asked. "Eyesore" was a bit of a stretch considering it was just the lawn that needed to be mowed.

"No, sorry. Just here to visit."

"Well, it doesn't appear as though anyone's home. Really needs to be, though... to clean this mess up," he muttered.

"Who are you exactly?" Jonas asked, sliding his jacket to the side to reveal the badge affixed to his waist.

"I'm code enforcement for the Borough. We've received complaints from neighbors regarding the overgrown vegetation. They are single-handedly bringing down the property values."

Jonas nodded while thinking how overly dramatic this man was being. "He might just be a little behind since he recently lost his wife and mother of his two sons."

"Hmmm... How unfortunate," he said flatly. "Well, he has a week to get it handled or he'll be receiving a citation," he replied matter-of-factly, shoving the written warning into his overstuffed mailbox.

"I'll remind him," Jonas offered as the man hopped into his work vehicle and pulled off.

When he was no longer in sight, Jonas rang the bell just in case Weston was, in fact, home but just not answering for that particular visitor. He listened closely to detect any signs of life coming from inside the home, but there were none.

Jonas walked around to one of the enormous windows at the front of the house and peered in, trying to see through the sheers, but there was no movement. He then peeked through the narrow garage window. Weston's Tesla was indeed there, parked beside another SUV concealed by a car cover. He tried the doorbell again, but when there was no answer, he left, thinking how odd it was to have a vehicle covered that was already inside a garage.

18

As Ruby felt her eyes opening, coming to once more, she still struggled to see with the darkness still enveloping her. It had to be another day by now, at least. There's no way it could still be the same night, could it?

As her consciousness gave way to the feelings of pain and prickles running down her entire left side, she began to breathe a little heavier in response. But with those deeper breaths, again, came those familiar smells. However, this time, it was mixed with the rancid odor of her own urine that she was covered in, still attached to the chair.

With her head pounding, she slowly came to the realization that she was no longer lying on her side. She recalled the chair tipping, but that's where the memories ended. She was again seated upright, which meant someone had been in that space with her.

He's still here. I can smell him. And food? She thought as her stomach angrily rumbled. *Is that McDonald's? Ugh, I fucking hate McDonald's.* But that didn't matter, she felt like it had been ages since she had consumed anything. She would attempt to wrestle and eat a live porcupine if given the option.

She could hear her dry mouth open as she attempted to speak. "Hello?"

Silence.

"I know you're in here," Ruby struggled to vocalize with her scratchy, dehydrated throat.

He was... seated directly in front of her, enjoying every moment of her anxiety, frustration, and... pain, watching through his night vision eyewear. He had accepted the money to get rid of her, but this part he was just doing for free... because it was fun for him.

"Reveal yourself, you loathsome coward!" she demanded with as much authority as she could, given her clearly submissive state. "Stop being a little bitch..." she mumbled dryly, forcing a parched swallow.

A bright light clicked on directly in front of her, instantly blinding her after being in total darkness for so long. She whimpered because that's all she could get out, immediately closing her eyes and turning her face away from the painful illumination.

Fucker!! she thought as she heard the light click off then out of nowhere, THWACK! She was struck across the face hard enough that the chair almost tipped over again. She painfully cried out, feeling blood begin to pool in her mouth. She didn't mean to scream, but it was so unexpected. Had she seen it coming, she could have braced for the impact and attempted to control her response to not give this asshole the reaction he so clearly enjoyed.

Part of her wanted to swallow the metallic-tasting accumulation because at least that would be some sort of fluid to coat her burning throat. But she elected to spit it forward in hopes of hitting her captor.

"You missed," the deep voice taunted before striking her again even harder.

The only thing that cut through the silence was Ruby gasping for breath, but she could also hear her ears ringing loudly. She did swallow that time and kept her mouth shut because she wasn't sure how many more times she could survive being hit in the head with that much force, unable to defend herself.

Her throbbing right eye began to sting as blood from that last strike seeped into it. She could feel it starting to swell right before the overhead light in the room quickly turned on, forcing her eyes shut once more from the brightness. But in that instant before they closed, she immediately recognized her surroundings.

You've got to be fucking kidding me right now.

Scared to keep her eyes closed for too long in fear of another unexpected assault, her eyes fluttered, struggling to acclimate to the brightness of the room. But every time her eyes even slightly parted, she saw the man nonchalantly sitting in front of her, watching her as cool as if he were sitting on the couch viewing Sports Center.

Once her eyes had fully adjusted, she gasped as he glared at her, standing to approach.

When she went to speak, he interrupted, "Drink."

Ruby was hesitant because when he turned the lid, she didn't hear it crack, which meant that wasn't a new bottle of water. Was it safe? Was it laced with something? It was a risk she would have to take because she needed that hydration immediately.

She stared up at him as she parted her lips to desperately accept the water he was offering, as much of it ran down her chin, soaking her shirt. It wasn't the bitter taste of it that made her feel like she was going to throw it all back up. It was when he started running his fingers through her hair while she drank that was more disgusting than the water.

When he stepped back, Ruby never took her glare off him. "How long have I been here?"

"Hmmm... About 36 hours."

That's it!? Fuck! Feels like so much longer... "You know they're looking for me, right?"

"I do. Your once beautiful face is plastered all over everyone's televisions. But I figured the very last place they would look is here. Who abducts someone and takes them back to their own house? The fact that you live out in the sticks made it make that much more sense."

"Weston, why are you doing this?" she begged, still incredibly weak after having not eaten for what she now knew to be two days.

"Such a silly question, Claudy. I missed you. Haven't you missed me?" he asked, squinting as he examined her bloodied caramel face. "Of course you didn't, because you were too busy fucking that animal in the window of his apartment!!" he suddenly yelled hysterically, wielding the black .38 caliber gun.

Weston took a deep breath to calm himself down. He cocked a tilted grin as he observed her eyes shifting around the room, clearly trying to devise a plan. What she didn't know was that he'd already found all of her weapons, boarded up the two windows in her master bedroom, and nailed all the rest of the windows shut. Death would be her only escape from this house.

Weston sat back in the chair across from her, set the gun on her nightstand behind him, and began to unwrap the food.

"Are you hungry, Claudy? Smells good, huh?" he asked, taking a huge bite in front of her. He could hear her stomach rumble in response, but she remained quiet, not wanting to give him the satisfaction of her discomfort.

"It's okay, Claudia," he replied, standing up. "You don't have to tell me, I can hear it," he taunted, glancing at her stomach. "You want some?" he questioned in a dark tone, towering over her. "Open your mouth."

Ruby was sickened by all the innuendo that dripped from that simple sentence, but she reluctantly complied as best she could, considering her jaw and the entire side of her face were actively swelling and throbbing. She pretty much had to swallow the small bites whole because chewing was like some new form of torture.

When he put the water bottle back up to her lips, she uttered, "What's in this water?"

Weston smiled with pride. His baby girl was so astute. "Just a little something to make you feel better. It'll help with the pain in your face... and everything else I'm going to do to you," he said, grabbing the back of her head and forcing the mysterious liquid down her throat until she choked and coughed some of it back up.

Chest heaving and struggling to catch her breath, Ruby glared at him as she pointlessly fought against the secure tethers. The irony was not lost on her that she should now be the one abducted and restrained. The same thing she'd done countless times to the others. *Is this some sort of twisted Karma? She really* is *a bitch.*

Just inches away from her face, he studied hers, then leaned in and whispered into her ear, "You're fucking disgusting. You stink."

Not nearly as much as your severed, decomposing head mounted above my fireplace will if I ever get out of here.

"Let's get you cleaned up!" he announced with some pep in his step as he made his way over to her chest of drawers. He laid out the purple satin nightie with see-through lace over the bust. He came across the matching panties, held them up with a smile, then looked to Claudia and said, "You won't be needing these."

Ruby rolled her eyes and looked away, thinking about how she would almost rather be waterboarded than have to endure the dreadfully boring sex with him... again. But it's not like she could do anything about it. In the past two days, all she had to sustain her were a few bites of a disgusting breakfast sandwich and enough water to coat her throat and drug her, but not enough to truly hydrate her. She was in so much pain and still so weak. And whatever was in that water was having a kind of euphoric effect. She wasn't drowsy, but she wasn't laser-focused either.

From behind, she could hear him open his switchblade and feel the blood flow to her lower extremities return when he sliced through the thin but sturdy rope and down the thick gorilla tape that had adhered her to that chair.

She grunted, trying her best to conceal her pain when he ripped the super sticky adhesive from her skin.

"Sorry," he smiled. "Let's go. Try anything funny and I will put two in your knees, lock you in this room, and leave you here to die a slow death."

"Wasn't that your plan anyway?" she mumbled through her tightened jaw that would barely open.

Weston chuckled as he led her to her en suite bathroom, where she noticed that he had removed her elegant cloth shower curtain, and all that remained was the clear shower liner. She caught her reflection in the huge mirror of the his-and-hers sink and quietly gasped. The right side of her face was almost unrecognizable and looked like she'd just gone toe to toe with Mike Tyson. Yet the left side looked perfectly untouched. She looked like two completely different people. It reminded her of the African painting she saw in Dr. Pearce's house, which she also ordered and never got to hang up. It was still on her dining room table.

He closed and locked the door, then took a seat on her toilet, resting the gun on his knee.

"Take off your clothes."

Ruby tilted her head and looked at him as if to say, seriously? "With one arm?"

Weston placed the gun on the back of the toilet, swiftly approached her, wrapped his sturdy hand around her neck, and jacked her up against the wall. If Ruby hadn't been in so much pain already, she likely would have enjoyed him ripping off her clothes with such haste and ferocity.

He reclaimed his seat and watched her enter the steaming hot shower while stroking his quickly growing erection.

As the water cascaded down her curvy body, Ruby noticed Weston had removed all her care essentials and left her with only a loofah, a washcloth, and a bar of cheap soap. None of her satin body washes, sugar scrubs, or facial cleansers, not that she would be able to do much with them anyway. She turned the lever to lower the temperature of the water so she could tend to her broken face while watching him pleasure himself at her painful expense.

What the fuck is wrong with him? It's not even like he knows how to use that thing anyway, she thought to herself while trying to drink some of the shower water without him noticing. She'd hoped that she could get enough in her to help flush out whatever he'd made her drink, but it was unlikely. Hell, she was even struggling to just stand steadily at that point.

"I umm... I need a razor," Ruby requested.

Weston genuinely laughed. "You think I'm going to give you a razor right now? That's cute. I'll take you au naturel," he said, putting himself back into his black Adidas sweatpants and jerking her out of the shower.

With as much force as she could, she elbowed him in the chin and tried to run across the bathroom to get to the sink, where she knew she had a weapon hidden so she could end this. In her mind, she was swift. But in real life, she was injured, dehydrated, and drugged, trying to run wet and barefoot on a tiled floor. She didn't actually stand a chance, which she realized when she hit the hard floor. She wasn't sure if she had slipped, or if her legs just gave out because of her current state of exhaustion.

Weston shifted his jaw back and forth, not expecting her to have that much force behind a blow. He towered over her, watching her slowly army crawl toward the sink as she grunted in frustration.

He roughly grabbed Ruby by her long curly hair, flipped her over and before losing consciousness again, she glimpsed his thick fist, still donning a platinum wedding ring, rushing toward her already broken face. After that blow, the blinding pain almost completely overshadowed the feeling of him forcefully parting her knees with his own and savagely entering her right there on the cold bathroom floor. The last thing she heard whispered into her ear was, "I already found your entire arsenal, you dumb bitch."

19

Higgins arrived to work early to find Maceo seated in the lobby.

"How long's he been here?" Higgins asked Teddy while glancing at his watch.

"No clue. He was there when I got here, so I don't know if he ever even left."

Higgins approached and sat down across from him. He observed Maceo's bloodshot, puffy eyes and the fact that he was still wearing the same clothes as the day before.

"Not gonna ask if you're okay. I already know the answer."

Mace barely nodded an acknowledgment. He had never felt so powerless in his entire life. And in his line of work, that was not a feeling to which he was accustomed. There was always something he could do, but in this situation, there wasn't. The only upside was if they really had found the Keeper, at least she would hopefully be located in one piece. Maceo had been canvassing the city on foot with her pictures in his phone asking if anyone had seen her. He was driving through obscure alleyways, just looking for... Anything. Any clue... But he didn't even know what.

Missing Persons was handling the search for Claudia in hopes of finding her before it ended up in the lap of Higgins' Violent Crimes Unit.

"Did they get the warrant for her devices yet?"

"They had one, but they didn't need it. I woulda let them in and gave them whatever they wanted. I just want her found, Cap."

He nodded, switching seats to the one beside Maceo to comfort him. "Did they get a warrant for her house?"

"I don't think so. If they did, they didn't mention it. She had been with me for the past almost two months and was abducted from my residence. Everything of importance was at my place."

He ruggedly wiped away a tear that began to form in the corner of his eye. "I feel like it's all my fault, man. It's like every time she's with me something bad happens."

"Maceo. You know you cannot blame yourself for her getting shot. And you *definitely* can't blame yourself for this."

"But if I hadn't gone to work that night-"

"And if the sky wasn't blue. And if dogs didn't bark... all the what ifs. You were doing your job - what you needed to do. We're going to place blame where it belongs, with the sick fuck who took her. And we're going to do everything we can to get her back."

Mace nodded in agreement.

"Go home, get a shower, and try to get some sleep. You're no good to anyone in this condition."

Mace exhaled sharply and nodded once more, knowing damn well there was no way he'd be able to just fall asleep as long as she was out there.

Detective Rainer arrived at the squad room to find a gift bag on her desk. She opened the card that simply read *RAVENS synonym: Dirty Bird*. She peeked in to find the brand-new thesaurus they'd joked about getting her.

"Ok, Burgess got jokes..." she chuckled, sliding the book into her desk. She had heard these guys on this squad could cut up with the best of them. She just didn't expect to be on the receiving end so quickly.

"Rainerrrr," Burgess sang, coming through the doors, with a bright smile. "I see you got my gift."

"I did," she smiled. "Though I don't necessarily appreciate you trash-talkin' my team."

"Okay, I'm not tryin' to start nothin'..."

"Good."

"But who won the last meet-up?" he teased.

Rainer thought about it, "*We* did actually."

Burgess opened his mouth, then closed it immediately. "Damn it, that's right."

"See. Just like you Steelers fans to be talkin' shit even when you're losing," she joked but was internally serious.

Burgess just smiled, nodded, and took that one because he knew she was right. Steeler Pride was damn near tangible.

"That's ok... We're comin' back."

"Y'all always are," she said, rolling her eyes.

"Okay guys," Higgins said, exiting his office and hustling through the squad room. "Just want what's happening next door on your radar. Yinz all heard on the news about the two men found shot in their cars in Beaver and Fayette Counties?"

"There was another? I just heard about the first," Rainer responded.

"Yup. Just putting it out there in case this person is just county hopping and ours is next. Their investigators are working together since the attacks have the same M.O. - victims found in their cars on back roads, bullet to the head at point-blank range, and made to look like a robbery."

"Made to look like?" Burgess asked. "The news said they *were* robbed."

"Technically, yes. Both passenger doors were left open, compartments were rifled through, and items of value were taken, but the passenger side interior wasn't wiped down. So, in Beaver, they found prints belonging to Dan Hogan's wife and children but no one else. They were able to rule out the wife as a suspect, so it's possible that someone got into this man's car wearing gloves, and if they did, it's more likely he would have been shot from the passenger side. Both men were shot by a person standing outside of the vehicle's driver's side."

"Right. That would mean that the shooter got out of the car, walked around to the driver's side, and then shot. And in that amount of time, what's to prevent the driver from pulling off to at least try to get away from this person? Which means that it wouldn't have been a point-blank shot and would have come more likely from behind."

"They also would have found the car wrecked and not parked," Burgess added.

"Exactly," Higgins stated. "But they pulled two sets of prints from the second victim's car yesterday that they are working to identify."

"Did they happen to tell you if there was anything special about these two men?"

"Special?" Higgins inquired, frowning.

"I mean... special like disturbed."

"Rainer. You know those two words are not-"

"Look Cap, we got her ass a thesaurus," Burgess interrupted jokingly. "Our work here is done."

Higgins shook his head at his detectives, browsing the files he'd been sent. "No, nothing mentioned. Dan Hogan was a musician with one of the local orchestras and taught piano. Jerry Marcuse was a school bus driver. What makes you ask about how... special they are?"

"Someone just robbed a musician and a part-time driver? Jerry drove a beat-up Honda for Pete's sake. If I want to rob someone and risk everything by killing them, wouldn't I at least wanna make sure I'm getting something substantial out of the deal by choosing a more affluent mark? There has to be something more in common between those men."

"You're probably right," Higgins acknowledged. "But these are not our cases. So, until a man shows up in our city limits matching this M.O., we focus on helping to find Martinez, figuring out this Kelly Knight overdose situation, and the string of dead young men found in the Ohio River."

"Burgess," he said as a greeting when answering his ringing phone. "Yup, send her up."

Burgess stood when Hope tentatively entered the squad room. At first glance, she appeared well put together, but upon closer inspection, the large puffy bags under her dark eyes told another story.

"Hi everyone. Sorry to interrupt," she said meekly. "I just stopped to see if there were any updates on my sister. I- I called Maceo but..."

"He was here early this morning. Not doing so hot," Higgins interrupted. "I sent him home. So hopefully he is getting the sleep that it looks like you probably need as well."

She nodded.

"Unfortunately, I don't have any updates of substance. I know they have her devices. They got a warrant to pull phone records to see who she's been talking to. Scouring her social media looking for any threats made," he said, glancing up at Detective Jonas Torrey, tracking him as he entered the squad room and made his way to his desk. He looked back over at Hope when she began to speak.

"Um... I know she had been staying with Maceo, but did anyone check her house?"

"I went out there, actually."

"I'm sorry, you probably haven't met Detective Denise Rainer yet."

"No, nice to meet you."

The rookie detective nodded back with an empathetic smile. "The mail was piled up and the house was dark inside. I peeped through the windows that I could but saw nothing suspicious, so I couldn't enter without a warrant."

Hope nodded. "Am I allowed to go collect her mail? I told her to have it forwarded. She is *so* damn stubborn," Hope murmured, trying to hold back tears.

"Of course," Rainer replied, approaching the distraught woman for reassurance.

She placed a hand on Hope's shoulder and gave it a comforting squeeze. With a consoling smile, she walked the shaken woman out of the office offering to answer whatever additional questions she could, along with a promise to keep her updated.

20

As her swollen eyes opened once more, only a small nightlight across the room provided any indication of her whereabouts. As her mind began to awaken, so did the pain that tore through her body. Her breathing shifted, trying to wake herself up from this torturous nightmare. This was a new one. She'd never had one like this before. Actually, she hadn't even had one since she realized what Miles had done to her. The painful throbbing between her legs clearly indicated that her stepdad had succeeded in this new nightmare.

Claudia instinctively opened her mouth to scream, but instead, a harsh moan crossed her lips when the pain of trying to move her jaw seared through the right side of her face.

"Hello?" she croaked, clearing her throat and trying to move, but her hands were numb from what felt like tight metal restraining her arms.

As she tried to disregard the pain to figure out what was happening, she started to realize that she was not actually dreaming, which caused panic to set in. Her mouth was so dry that she immediately thought it best to stop her fearful panting and breathe through her nose instead.

"Helloo," she cried out once more... at least she thought she did. Her head hurt so badly.

She realized that every time she moved, there was a clanking noise that also felt like it was drilling into her skull. But maybe it was loud enough to alert someone to her presence, so she kept trying to move.

When the bedroom door swung open and the lights flipped on, it took a few seconds for her to adjust, but her eyes widened once she did.

"Oh my gahhh, Weston!" she breathed heavily with relief. "Thank God it's you! Please, get me outta- I-" she moaned in a frantic but weakened state. "I don't know what... Help..."

With her one good eye, she watched the man she loved saunter over to her way too casually considering her predicament. Why was he not as shocked to find her in this situation as she was to wake up *in* it? And why was he so much larger? She felt like she had *just* seen him the other day. Everything was so fuzzy as she struggled to remember... anything. *Ugh! I got out of the shower... ummm... put on Weston's t-shirt - smelled like him... Uhhh Tanner! He came over... then what? Did I sleep with Tanner again, and Weston found out? Unnnghh.... there were woods... Why was I in the woods? How'd I get here!?*

He stood at her bedside, glaring down at her with her arms splayed, tightly restrained to her thick, ornate, metal bed frame. "What kind of game are you trying to play here, Claudia?"

Fear and total confusion could be seen in that one eye and on the part of her face that she could control.

"I don't-" her breathing deepened as her salty tears cascaded through the open wounds on her face. "What's..." she panted faster, realizing that *he* was the reason she was tied to her *own* bed. "Why are you doing this?" she painfully mumbled between sobs.

Weston squinted then frowned staring down at her. She looked so fearful and innocent, unlike the raging bitch he fought in the bathroom a few hours ago. Something was up.

"Drink."

Claudia was so thirsty but turned her head away. "Just let me out of here, please, Weston," she begged. "Tell me what happened! Tell me- aaaghhh," she grunted and cried when he delivered a solid backhand to shut her up and stop her from trying to manipulate him. She was suddenly so emotional whereas just yesterday, she fought tooth and nail not to let him see even a sliver of weakness. And she didn't even have the same harsh wickedness in her eyes that he had previously seen. What kind of game was she playing? He was determined not to be swayed by her, but he almost felt bad hearing her sob in agony when he grabbed her chin, forced her face back toward him, and made her drink his special water.

Weston could see the fear and confusion in her eyes. But then, he remembered all the times he had watched her with Maceo... heard them having what sounded like the most mind-blowing sex... the fact that he risked his job for her and murdered his wife... all for this slut! It constantly replayed in his head, causing him to strike her once more to get the rage out.

"What... did I... do..." Claudia uttered between tortured wails. "Weston... *please*..."

"You know damn well what you did, you filthy whore. Now it's time to pay," he whispered ominously, opening her nightstand and removing the olive-green tie that she had given him.

Claudia shook her head no, pleading with him not to hurt her anymore.

Weston knotted the silk tightly around her bicep, then pulled a syringe from his back pocket. "Time for your medicine, baby."

"Nooo..." Claudia protested miserably through quiet tears, powerless to stop him as he injected the clear fluid directly into her bloodstream.

Her entire body completely relaxed as all the pain she felt immediately subsided. Whatever he'd administered made her limbs feel heavy. She could move, but very minimally even though it felt like her body was floating. She was completely conscious and could feel and hear everything around her, but it was very difficult to keep her eyes open - they were just so heavy. At least most of the pain dissipated though.

Claudia shifted her weary eyes to watch Weston unlock the cuff on her left hand and she felt it drop heavily onto the bed beside her. She mumbled incoherent objections, watching him pull down his pants and step out of them before her gaze shifted up to meet his, silently imploring him not to do this.

For a moment, Weston paused. Claudia thought she had finally gotten through to him until he climbed into bed beside her and coldly turned her onto her side so he wouldn't have to look at her.

With his body pressed closely against hers from behind, he felt Claudia stiffen and hold her breath, which made him stop momentarily, and then he heard it too - tires on gravel.

Weston immediately jumped out of bed, slid back into his sweatpants, and ran around to the other side of the bed to face Claudia, still lying on her side. Her right arm was still attached to the bed frame, so he maneuvered her pillow between her arm and her head to conceal the restraint. He slid the sheet up and then kissed her limp, lifeless lips. "I'm going to take care of whoever is outside, and then we can finish up here. You be my good girl and don't make a sound, or Daddy's going to have to punish you again."

21

As Hope stepped out of her car, she zipped up her coat then stood for a few moments looking at her sister's property. Claudia was usually good about maintaining her landscaping, but it had been months since she had been home. Hope loved the fact that Claudia was so much closer to her at Maceo's place. She began to get emotional thinking about the fact that she had no idea where her only sister was or if she was even alive.

Weston was crouched down behind the kitchen island watching Hope on his phone via the hidden camera he'd mounted. *What the hell is she doing? Why is she just standing there? Just leave!* His heart was racing because this was not part of the plan. Had he just done what he was supposed to and killed Claudia, he and his boys could have been together at the non-extradition location he'd selected by now. Instead, he decided to send them to be with Alessandra's parents in Italy so he could have his fun torturing her before mutilating and killing her. His heart was pounding as he panted nervously, waiting to see what she'd do or where she'd go. Worse come to worst, he had no problem murdering her with Maceo's gun.

His breathing began to regulate when he watched Hope collect all of Claudia's mail that was overflowing her box and piled up beside her door. She loaded it up in the trunk, took one last look at the house, then got into her car.

Weston chuckled at that very close call as his heart rate decelerated. He was so glad that she wasn't feeling nosy because his car was surely parked in the garage that Claudia seldom used. He stood up relaxing further, then his mind shifted to his lady who was currently lying in their bed pantiless in that sexy, purple lace waiting just for him. She was all *his* now.

He set his phone on the kitchen island only to notice Hope on the screen getting back out of the vehicle and making her way to the front door holding a lanyard full of keys.

Oh shit!

Hope stood in front of Claudia's door sifting through the keys on her keychain. "The police might need a warrant, but damn it, I don't," she muttered. She was positive Claudia had given her the new key, but she couldn't seem to find it. Had she lost it somewhere?

Maybe it's this one, she thought as she opened the screen door and inserted the key into the hole. She tried to turn it back and forth, but nothing. Hope stood sifting through additional keys, thinking about how when she found her sister, she would have to tell her that she'd lost the key to her house. Because they were *going* to find her. And she was *going* to be okay.

With no idea that Ruby had removed it from her lanyard the last time she visited, Hope continued trying different keys, even though she was fairly certain those weren't the ones.

She could see her breath coming out in frustrated puffs as she put her mittens back on to protect her hands from the cold.

As Hope stepped back to assess the front of the house once more, thinking maybe Claudia *did* end up re-hiding the key even though she said she wouldn't, she jumped when a figure suddenly emerged.

Hope gasped in shock because she wasn't expecting her missing sister's door to just swing open. "Weston?" she asked in disbelief when she finally got her bearings about her.

He stood in Claudia's doorway wearing nothing more than a warm smile and a pair of light gray Adidas sweatpants, his chest bare and very well sculpted. *Oh wow*, Hope thought. Weston had finally cleaned himself up for his lady, so his thick salt and pepper facial hair was perfectly sculpted and his hair slightly mussed, giving sultry, after-sex vibes.

A million and a half thoughts ran through Hope's mind as this seemingly much larger sexy man stood smiling at her like nothing was wrong. Had her sister just left Maceo to be with Weston and not told anyone? The whole world was worried sick and she's up here getting her cheeks clapped... not answering her phone...

"What are you doing here?" she asked.

He smirked and glanced down then back up at her. Instinctively she glanced down as well then gasped and immediately averted her eyes from the long bulge visible beneath his sweats.

"Umm... So, Claudia's been *here*... with *you*... all this time..." Hope assessed, growing increasingly annoyed at her sister's flagrant irresponsibility.

"Of course," he smiled. "Thought she would've said something, but come on in," he offered warmly, holding the door open for her. "She saw you on the camera, so she's in the back putting on some clothes."

Hope slowly approached the door.

"Don't worry, I'll go throw some clothes on too," Weston chuckled.

She smiled back tentatively, slowly entering the home. Part of her was relieved that Claudia was okay, but the other part of her was eight shades of pissed that she just vanished for over a week and said nothing. Then confusion entered the picture because seeing her sister with Maceo, they looked so happy together. Now her ex is answering her door half-naked? Then she started to wonder if Maceo's talk of marriage had scared her commitment-phobic sister back into Weston's arms. Either way, she was going to get a good talking to.

Hope removed her mittens as Weston closed and deadbolted the door behind them. "So, what happened with-"

"Oh, Mace?" Weston interjected. "Yeah, they had a huge fight," he explained, sliding the chain lock back into place.

"Oh... She hadn't mentioned anything," Hope stammered, looking around. "Why is it so cold in here?"

"Is it? I hadn't really noticed because, well, Claudy and I have been doing a great job keeping each other warm, if ya know what I mean," he winked. "Have a seat and make yourself comfortable. I'm sure she'll be out in a moment. Here ya go," he said, removing the lid and handing her a bottle of strawberry lemonade from Claudia's refrigerator.

"Thank you."

Weston smiled leaning against the counter as she took a seat at the island and a few long gulps. "So tell me, how's the family? I believe Claudy said she had two nephews?"

"Oh uhh... Yeah, the boys are good," she said awkwardly to the scantily clad man asking about her children. "Growing up fast." She turned her head to look down the hall at the still-closed bedroom door, wondering what was taking her sister so long.

"I can attest to that," he replied warmly. "My twins... Feels like I was just giving them their first bath and now they're so independent. They uh... they miss their mom though," he admitted sadly, using the topic of children and loss to put Hope more at ease.

"Yeah, I'm truly sorry to hear about the accident. My condolences," Hope offered, furtively glancing down the hall once more. "You know what? I'm just gonna go down and see what's taking her so long."

Weston calmly smiled and nodded.

Hope quickly made her way down the hall past the guest rooms toward the master suite. She felt a little off, but she attributed it to not having breakfast and being so worried about her sister but glad that she was okay. She just wanted to lay eyes on her.

In her bed, Claudia could hear a light tapping on her door, then her eyes widened when she heard her sister's voice on the other side, "CoCo?"

Nooooo

"I'm coming in."

She opened the door to find Claudia lying in bed in a fetal position, such that she couldn't see the damage to her sister's face. In the dimly lit room, it simply appeared as though she was peacefully sleeping in cute nightwear with her curls strewn about the pillow.

Hope ran over, relieved to see her baby sister. She tapped on the nightstand lamp beside them and kneeled, rubbing Claudia's arm to wake her when she immediately noticed how pale her skin was and that something was seriously wrong. *Shit.*

Claudia's left eye opened ever so slightly, and she mumbled something.

Hope's face was etched with concern, and her frown and lean-in indicated that she couldn't make out what Claudia had said.

"Runnn..." she barely whispered.

Hope gasped in terror as she instantly jumped up pulling her phone out of her pocket. She looked over to find Weston leaning in the bedroom doorway, impassively pointing a gun in her direction. "Well, that's just not a good idea. Put the phone on the bed."

Hope did as she was told and put her hands up. "Weston please, you don't want to do this. She's hurt."

"Hurt? No. That's just a little post-coital nap. She's a freak - she likes it rough. But she's fine."

Claudia repeatedly opened her eyes for as long as she could before they would heavily fall closed again.

"She's not fine! Please, we don't have to say anything, just let me get her help," she pleaded.

"I *am* helping her," he replied calmly, then his voice rising. "I'm helping her to gain a deeper understanding of why it's not okay to be a *manipulative slut!!*"

Claudia shuddered when the gun fired, knocking her sister back into the nightstand lamp and onto the floor. She cried as she watched Weston stand over her and check her vitals.

He turned toward Claudia with a sneer. "She's still alive." Then his smile slowly faded. "Not for much longer though."

Instead of simply firing once more and putting Hope out of her misery, Weston casually walked around, set the gun on the other nightstand, and climbed back into bed with her. With one hand around her neck, he savagely forced himself into her from behind while her sister lay bleeding out beside her on her bedroom floor. And there was nothing she could do about it.

By the time Weston was done, whatever he had given her had started to wear off slightly, just enough for her to start to feel the pain her body was going to be in. She heard

Hope stop struggling for breath what felt like a while ago. But she had no concept of time anymore.

As Weston aggressively restrained her left arm back to the bed, he observed her puffy, red, bloodshot eyes and tear-soaked hair.

"Why are you crying, Claudy? It's ok. I'm going to take care of Hope for you. See, I know what you're thinking," he said, stroking her inner thigh.

She tried to move her leg away from him, but it felt like it was made of concrete. She wanted to yell at him not to touch her, but at the same time, she didn't want to get punched again. He was so angry, and she still didn't know why.

He continued, "You're thinking that once they realize Hope is missing, they'll trace her phone, and it will lead them here. Then they'll find and rescue you. But that's where you're wrong. It'll take them a good eight more hours to notice she's missing and probably not till the next day to get moving on her."

"She's my sister..." Claudia faintly uttered. "I'm a cop... who's missing... she'll be... a priority."

"Even if she is, they still have to get the warrant for the phone, do all the pulling and tracing, and by the time they finally find her..." Weston smiled deviously like he knew something she didn't.

"Please," Claudia implored once more. "Just... tell me... why," she mumbled between labored breaths.

Weston stared down at her. Why did she look so confused? What game was she fucking *playing* here? Whatever it was, he was tired of it.

"I- I don't under- aaaghh!" He struck her again before she could even finish the sentence.

"Filthy slut. You know whyyy!!" he shouted, full of rage.

Before she knew it, he was pulling that green tie securely around her arm once more and injecting her again. Her heavy lids slowly falling closed caused the tears that were in her eyes to trickle down her face as she despondently watched Weston drag Hope's lifeless body out of her bedroom before passing out once more.

22

Higgins stormed out of his office, "Everyone! Stop everything," he huffed. "Just got a call from Moon Township PD. Missing person. Not our case, but it's Claudia's sister, Hope. Reported by her husband who returned home early from a business trip when his mother eventually notified him that Hope hadn't picked up the children. Last seen a little over 48 hours ago by her when she dropped them off. Her phone was still on and tracked all the way to Michigan before it either died or was turned off."

"Michigan!?" Burgess blurted in shock with the rest of the team.

"Yeah. They said it pinged in our area, then in the vicinity of Claudia's house."

"Which must be when she went to get her sister's mail," Rainer noted.

"It was in that vicinity for about forty minutes."

"Wait, forty minutes to get the mail?" Rainer pondered doubtfully.

"You went out there," Torrey replied. "You saw how long it took from any normal road just to get to her. Half of that time could have just been driving within the vicinity of the cell tower that's closest to her."

"True."

"So, the phone left Claudia's general area and pinged quickly off towers heading toward Beaver County, down the parkway. It eventually made it to the turnpike, and the last ping was in Ypsilanti, Michigan."

"So we think whoever has Claudia has *her*? She doesn't seem like the type to just leave her kids voluntarily," Torrey acknowledged.

"No clue. And we can't track Claudia's cell because it wasn't on her when she went missing."

The captain reached for his vibrating phone, "Higgins… Got it, thanks… Sending my people."

Ending the call, he announced, "The GPS puts her Nissan Rogue right off the Aliquippa exit. Rainer, get over there. Aliquippa PD knows to expect us."

"Cap, lemme ride."

"No. Burgess, go with," Higgins ordered.

"Cap!" Torrey said, coming from around his desk. "You know I ain't have nothin' to do with Claudia's disappearance, right?"

"No. I don't. Me awaiting more evidence and giving you the benefit of the doubt is the only reason you haven't been hauled into one of these interrogation rooms already," Higgins quietly hissed. "Now handle this," he bellowed, loudly dropping a thick file onto Torrey's desk before stomping away.

When Burgess and Rainer made it out to Aliquippa, the police and the crime scene unit had just finished blocking off the area.

"Detectives Eric Burgess and Denise Rainer. Pittsburgh."

"Detective Rafael Angelos. Nice to meet you."

"So just the car?"

"I wish. When they located the vehicle of the missing woman-"

"Hope. Her name is Hope," Rainer interrupted.

"Right, so when they found Hope's car, they looked into the windows after calling it in to be impounded until we could get a warrant. But when they peeked into the window of her trunk, that's where they saw her body, so we didn't have to wait for the warrant."

"Shit," Burgess muttered under his breath, squeezing his eyes shut and rubbing them. "Are you *absolutely* sure it's her? Her sister is also missing,"

"There's no mixing those two up. They're not even close to the same complexion. It's her. But you're welcome to go verify."

Rainer and Burgess made their way under the canopy erected to cover the car from additional snow flurries and introduced themselves to the coroner. He was about to begin removing the body, which sadly was indeed Hope's, from the trunk.

"At first glance, cause of death appears to be the gunshot wound to the lower abdomen. There's not much blood here though, so she either bled out at another location or the bullet hit an intestine causing sepsis. Identifying the exact time of death will be a little trickier considering the frigid temperature and the fact that she'd been inside the car, which pretty much acts as a cooler in these temps."

"So how the hell did her phone end up from here to Michigan?" Rainer probed, blowing her warm breath into her hands, then stuffing them into her pockets and bouncing to keep warm.

"There." Burgess eyed the three 18-wheelers barreling down the hill and taking the exit onto the parkway. "This is a major truck delivery area with all the factories and plants. It would be nothing to toss her phone onto one of these trucks and let it ride."

"Okay, but if someone left her car here, they had to get home... or wherever."

"Yeah... Uber? Lift?"

"Would you be dumb enough to murder someone, leave their body on the side of the road, and then call an Uber?"

"I mean, *I* wouldn't. But not all killers are smart, so we can check just in case. In this *particular* situation, I would've simply attached my car to that tow hitch there," he pointed out on her SUV. "Dropped it off, then disappeared."

"But that's assuming the killer has a smaller vehicle than her Rogue."

"Hey, can you make sure you also dust that tow hitch for prints as well, please?" Burgess asked the tech.

"Not a problem."

"If the killer rode down the parkway to take this exit and leave her car here, he had to have been caught on numerous cameras along I-376."

"Unless the bastard got off early and took the back roads," Rainer replied.

"Won't know 'til we take a looksie. Let's roll."

23

As Maceo readied himself to head into the office, he wondered how he was supposed to be even remotely effective. How did parents who were missing children function? The bills didn't stop just because a tragedy occurred. Someone still had to make money, and how was one supposed to focus on that when all they could think about is if their loved one would ever be brought home safely?

He missed the smell of her hair when he would cuddle with her in the middle of the night, usually against her will, but he suspected she was coming to enjoy it... the way she smirked but refused to laugh at his corny jokes. She wasn't fake. If it wasn't funny, she wasn't going to laugh, so when she did, he reveled in it. He couldn't stop thinking about the way she sashayed around the house in those cute little panties and how sexy she looked in his shirts. The way her mysterious hazel eyes took him in... Her soft lips... And now he had to go to work with every part of her on his mind. The director had given him some additional paid time off that he hadn't accrued, but it wasn't indefinite.

On his way out, he stopped at the framed image of them on the dresser. Then his mind shifted to Hope and the news story from last night about her body being found in the trunk of her car. This was a nightmare. She had a husband and two beautiful children who adored her. She didn't deserve an end like that. All he could do was pray that they didn't find Claudia next.

His thoughts were interrupted by the apartment intercom buzzing.

Mace hit the button to answer, "Hello?"

"Good morning, Mr. James. There are some detectives here to see you. Shall I send them-"

"Nah, here I come," he interrupted, grabbing his items and rushing out of the apartment.

On the elevator ride down, he put on his black shoulder holster over his button-down dress shirt and slid into his suit jacket, giving Will Smith/*Bad Boys* vibes - part of what made him and his girl look so hot together out in the field.

Maceo rushed over to the suited officers, "Agent Maceo James. You have news about Claudia?" he asked nervously.

"No, sorry. I'm Detective Rafael Angelos and we're here about Hope Jacobs-Turner."

"Hope?"

"Yes. Would you mind coming with us to the station please?"

Mace glanced among the three of them, all stone-faced, awaiting his reply.

Here we go again. "Am I under arrest?"

"No sir, you are not. We just have some questions that we hope can clarify a few things and help locate Detective Martinez."

That's all he needed to hear. "Y'all care if I just follow?"

"Not a problem."

On the ride out to Beaver County, he notified Director Yeager of what was going on, then tried to figure out why they would want to speak to him about Hope and how any of that would help them locate Claudia.

His stomach churned in the interrogation room waiting for the detective to finally join him. He also wondered how many people were behind the mirror watching. They were in a small-town police station, so probably not too many.

"Thank you for joining us, Agent James," Detective Angelos began, entering the overly lit room. "This is Detective Kenya Myer. She's joining us from Moon Township PD."

"Nice to meet you," she greeted cordially with a firm handshake.

As he sat down, Maceo could feel Kenya's deep sultry gaze on him, but he was less concerned about that and more concerned that two different police departments had joined forces to question him, which meant there were probably more people behind that glass than he'd originally thought.

"So, as you know," Angelos continued, "We recently located the body of Hope Jacobs-Turner in the trunk of her vehicle right off the Aliquippa exit here."

Maceo nodded sadly and exhaled.

"How many guns do you have registered?"

"Four. Plus my service pistol, but that's registered to the City of Pittsburgh."

"Why didn't you report any of them missing?"

With a confused look, he countered, "Because they're not."

"So, you claim to be in possession of all of your firearms?"

"Of course."

His response didn't instill much confidence because he was thinking when he said it. He knew for a fact he had one in his shoulder holster, one on his ankle, and the third hidden deep in his car's center console. The other two were at the house.

"Then can you explain this?" Angelos questioned, sliding a crime scene image of a firearm lodged between the rungs of a storm drain as though someone went to drop it in but didn't verify that it had gone down. "We found it near where Mrs. Jacobs-Turner's body was… deposited."

Maceo's eyes widened, then shifted all over the place thinking about how his gun could have ended up at a crime scene where his girlfriend's sister was found murdered.

"We know this gun is registered to you. And once they run ballistics, what are the odds that you think it will match this weapon?"

"It's mine," he verified heavily. "But I… don't know how it got… there."

"So, you're saying that your missing girlfriend's sister was murdered with your gun, and you have no idea how it happened?"

Maceo crossed his arms. "That's *exactly* what I'm sayin'. Are y'all serious right now? I'm an FBI agent. You think I would leave a body stuffed in a trunk on a busy highway and then leave my gun that close to it?"

Angelos returned the image to the manila envelope.

"And look at it! That gun has a chrome mirror finish with a pearlized grip. It's stunning. And expensive! So, I'm murdering someone with the most conspicuous gun I own and dropping it in a storm drain? I need everyone in the room and behind the glass to use any bit of common sense."

Maceo sighed... "It's the mayor," he mumbled, shaking his head. "She is somehow behind this."

"The *mayor*," Detective Myer repeated skeptically.

He sighed and placed his palms on the table. "Look, you can verify with FBI Director Anthony Yeager, their profiler Agent Weston Grant, and Lieutenant Joseph Hasting that that bitch, Audra Conrad, had me arrested. Had me pulled from a job, cuffed, and dragged into the station like a common criminal."

"We don't see that anywhere in your record."

"Of course you don't. Because it was all bogus. Look. She tried to hire me to kill Detective Martinez. When I declined, she tried to set me up for some other shit to destroy my credibility if it became my word against hers. I know that bitch has something to do with Claudia being taken. And it wouldn't shock me at all if she had something to do with murdering Claudia's sister as payback. Bring *her* ass in!"

"We would gladly pick her up if we could," Detective Myer replied casually, "But that bitch, as you called her, is dead," she divulged, pulling a crime scene photo from the file.

Maceo's stomach twisted into several knots.

"Killed with the same sized bullet as the one they removed from Hope's body interestingly enough. And now that you have referred to the late mayor as a bitch several times and informed us that you suspect she abducted your girlfriend over some past vendetta, we're thinking they're both going to match this gun."

"Look. They can match that gun all they want, but I'm not the one who fired it - either time! That's the weapon I keep in the center console of my vehicle. Obviously, someone stole it."

"That's your story?"

"Damn right," he asserted, standing and yanking his suit jacket off the back of the chair, fully intending to leave since he wasn't under arrest. "Let me know when you find the *real* killer."

"Don't plan on leaving town for a while, Agent James," Angelos shouted as Mace angrily stormed down the hall and out of the building.

24

Claudia had no idea how much time had passed since the man she once loved murdered her sister. She watched him do it. So, there was no doubt in her mind that he was going to kill her as well when he was done torturing her. She just wished he'd get it over with already.

The psychological aspect was almost worse than the physical. At least physically, she could try to zone out and go somewhere else until he was done. But leaving her alone for hours on end in the freezing, pitch-black room was something she couldn't just mentally escape from as much as she tried. Cold weather sometimes came early in Pittsburgh, so by now, her heat would normally be on. And it was. She could hear it click on and off, but he had covered all the vents in the room. Her fingers and toes were numb, and if she had any light, she would swear she could see her breath. He also covered the vents in the bathroom, forcing her to step naked out of a warm shower onto an ice-cold floor in a frigid room. He even removed the area rugs. All this made her think was, *is this what they trained them for in the FBI?*

He had switched out her soft-watt bulbs to the brightest light bulbs ever made. She had dimmer switches on all the lights. He *could* ease them on if he wanted, but the sadistic side of him was reveling in her pain and suffering, so he would flip them on fully and then force her eyes open.

During each visit, Weston would only ever feed her breakfast. It could have been dinnertime, but he was feeding her breakfast. She had had so many breakfasts that she didn't know how many days she had actually been gone. It felt like months... Could it have been? Pittsburgh stays cold through March.

Every time he came in, it was the same merciless routine. The bitter water laced with who knows what. The breakfast. The shower. The rape, which he referred to as their "lovemaking." The drugs, rather, her "medicine" as he called it. It was happening so often that she wasn't sure if the days were just going by that quickly or if he was doing this multiple times a day just to mess with her head.

He was feeding and watering her with just enough to keep her body functioning and providing just enough of whatever was in that syringe to take the edge off her pain briefly. She could tell he'd been increasing the dosage because it felt like it was lasting longer.

At first, she would beg him not to inject her, but once he had, it felt so good, and it took the care away. It helped her zone out and didn't hurt as badly when he was inside of her afterward. But then, out of nowhere, he just reversed the order, making her agree to their "lovemaking" before she could have her "medicine." He would take his time with her, drawing out their "love" session when all she wanted was for him to make the pain end.

He had finally stopped hitting her... Well, except for that first time when he reversed the order of the sex and the drugs. When she was high, she was far less aware of how brutal, aggressive, and painful it was. When she began to cry, he started hitting her again, yelling about how she never cried when Maceo fucked her like this. Who the hell was Maceo? He continued battering her, roaring at her to stop crying as if continually thrashing her was going to help with that. He wanted her to sound like she did when she was with Maceo.

So, she moaned for him. However, they were moans of torment and trying to hold back tears. But Weston was so engrossed in what he was doing it all sounded the same to him. Then he would inject her, sending her into a blissful peace. She was no longer aware of the stinging sensation ripping through her lower body or her entire face, which happened to be missing two of her side teeth. Do you know how hard you have to punch someone to loosen and eventually knock out molars? Not to mention the fact that her jaw, much like her arm, still had a very limited range of motion.

What also seemed to lessen his physical violence was that she finally stopped asking him why he was doing this to her. That always triggered a vengeful eruption like she was intentionally playing dumb, when she legitimately had no idea why any of this was happening. Last she could remember, she was waiting for him to leave Alessandra so they could be together. And now he was holding her captive in her own house, getting her strung out on drugs.

Weston entered the room, and for the first time, he eased on the overhead lights. It got to the point where she was looking forward to him visiting, not only for human interaction but also for the shower. It was the only time she got any warmth, and she was so thirsty.

After feeding and watering her like the captive animal she was, he sat down on the bed beside her instead of immediately loosening the restraint on her left leg and her right arm. He had finally started leaving the other arm unrestrained because he knew how damaged it was and that there was very little she could do with it in terms of escaping or defending herself.

"My... shower?" Claudia inquired softly.

He looked her up and down and smiled. He knew she didn't need one, as they had just gone through this routine about seven hours ago. But she didn't know that. "You want one today?"

"Yes... please..." she mumbled hopefully.

Because she asked so nicely, he was feeling generous and allowed her the warmth of the shower before putting her frail, bruised body into a cute daffodil-colored nightie.

He could see she was on the verge of tears as he tightly restrained her left leg, but she was a good girl and held it in.

"Please, Weston," Claudia begged. "Can you just... leave my arm free? My foot is cuffed, I can't go anywhere. Please?"

"You've been so well-behaved lately that, under normal circumstances, I would," he said as he gently pulled her arm up to the top corner of the bed to cuff it. "I mean, if I'm being totally honest, I miss feeling you run your fingers through my hair while I taste you. But it's time for me to go."

Claudia's eyes enlarged nervously.

"You see," Weston said, stroking her hair and running his fingers down her body. "They found your sister. A trace of her phone will show that this was her last location before going M.I.A. So, they'll eventually get a warrant. As much as I tried, I'm certain I didn't avoid every single camera on my way to dumping her vehicle and body. So, it's only a matter of time before someone somehow connects Alessandra's car to me, and I prefer not to be in the country when they do. I was supposed to kill you and be living my best life in Montenegro a long time ago. But honestly, I feel like *not* mounting your pretty little head on a stick and allowing you to starve to death is a far greater punishment for the anguish you've caused. Conrad would probably object to me leaving you alive, but since she *isn't* anymore, it's all good, Babydoll," he gushed in an icky sweet tone.

Claudia stared up at him not only in fear but also confusion because she wanted *so* badly to ask, but she knew he would strike her again.

He leaned in and whispered to her, "Do you know what they *do* to cops in prison?"

A tear streaming down her face, she quietly uttered, "Why would I... go to..." But she stopped when she saw his facial expression darken. "*Please*. Don't leave me here!"

"It's okay, baby. You won't be here too much longer. Your team will eventually get here for you. It's just that you probably won't be alive when they do." he taunted, gently kissing her on the forehead and then turning to walk away.

"*Wait!*"

Weston stopped and turned back around.

"Can... I..." she breathed heavily, looking at his pocket from where he normally kept her 'medicine.' "Please..."

He smiled, returning to her bedside.

Claudia was so thankful because she could already feel her body needing it.

"Well, you know what *I* get if you want your 'medicine,' right?" he asked, running his middle finger up her inner thigh.

She disgustedly turned her head away and sharply inhaled, holding in the tears. She nodded her head, while slowly sliding her unrestrained right leg open as an unwelcome invitation.

Weston "made love" to her for the last time, almost like he was *trying* to force cries so he would have an excuse to hit her once more as well, but she held strong knowing that as soon as he was done, he would make the pain go away. She could have her "medicine" and wouldn't have to endure this horror anymore.

"Good girl," Weston said, kissing her neck and cleavage before climbing off her once perfect, but now tainted body.

Her breathing became slightly more rapid as she anxiously anticipated him tying the infamous green tie around her arm and sending her into ecstasy.

Once he put himself back together, he set one miniature bottle of water on the bed beside her, another on the nightstand, and then pulled the full syringe out of his pocket.

He watched her body twitch with anticipation, and it mildly annoyed him that she responded more favorably to the "medicine" in that syringe than to him "making love" to her. But he smiled tenderly as he securely wrapped the tie around her arm and then gently placed the syringe on the nightstand beside the extra water, *well* out of her reach.

"Wha- what are you- NOO!!!" Claudia growled, twisting her body against the restraints. "I need my medicine!! *Weston! Please!!! I need it*! I gave you what you wanted you sick fuck!! It's not fair!!" She screamed, cried, and swore at him, yelling for him to not leave her like this. "*Wait!* I'm sorry! *Please,* Weston baby! I'll do whatever you want, just *please!*"

Weston grinned as he turned off her lights and closed the door, deserting Claudia once again in icy pitch blackness.

As he casually strolled down the hall to exit her house, he could hear her agonizing wails and tormented bawling. He felt at peace about the fact that going through the withdrawal alone might just kill her. *Let's see how you like going crazy, desperately wanting the one thing in the world that lies just beyond your reach that you can't have.*

25

That fucker left me to die, she thought, trembling in the frigid dark room with no idea if or when anyone would ever find her. She had no grasp of how long it had been, but it felt like days already.

He left *one* bottle of his special bitter water within her reach, which he had to know she would drink immediately in an effort to alleviate the pain she was feeling from the withdrawal. She tried to drink it sparingly, but she was already so incredibly dehydrated, and her throat was raw from screaming at Weston, begging him not to leave her... at least without making her feel good. So she couldn't help but to pretty much down that water. Within minutes, she was vomiting violently from whatever new drug he'd laced that water with, likely to intentionally cause that exact result.

If I can just shake my body enough to shift the bed across the floor to get closer to the nightstand, I can reach it...
"Ugghhh...." she grunted, shifting and shaking what she could of her body, praying that the bed was moving closer. After trying in vain and horrific pain to reach her bad arm

across her body, Claudia slowly realized that it didn't matter how close she got to the nightstand; if she was even close at all, she would not be able to reach her "medicine."

"Aaaaagghhh..." she viciously yelled in futility because all that did was fatigue her further. Her wrist had begun to bleed from trying to pull it out of the handcuff to get to that syringe, which only caused additional pain.

Claudia's body was covered in sweat, violently trembling as her heart raced due to her elevated blood pressure from the withdrawal. She moaned desperately in agony because every muscle in her body twitched and ached.

I want to diiie! Please, just let me die already! I'm sooo cold...

She hadn't heard the heat click on in the house at all since Weston had left. It felt like days, but it couldn't have been because she was still alive, and you can only survive a few days without water. *What could I possibly have done to deserve any of this? I just want to die...*

She wailed out in pain when her bladder released, and it felt like a dozen needles had just exited her body, burning and stinging so badly. Her entire lower region was ripped and raw from the savage sexual abuse that Weston had inflicted what seemed like multiple times per day. She knew she had a urinary tract infection from the number of times Weston had "made love" to her and wouldn't let her use the bathroom afterward. The one time she'd done it right there in the bed was the one time he'd beaten and sodomized her while holding her face down in it like a dog being punished for peeing in the house. Once he realized how much he enjoyed her back entrance, and she didn't, he did it much more often. She was oblivious before because the drugs took the pain away.

Her entire core throbbed from a combination of hunger pains and nausea. Several times, she turned to vomit over the right side of the bed but since Weston had only fed her enough food to keep her alive, not much came up. But that didn't stop her from dry heaving anyway, which made the pounding in her head unbearable. What was even worse was the diarrhea caused by her not being able to get her hands on that medicine - it was quite literally the cure for her entire illness.

To vomit over the side of the bed was one thing, but to be forced to lie in her own urine and fecal matter that exited her body like water was beyond degrading. How humiliating would it be when they finally found her covered in her own bodily waste?

How could he do this to me!? She gasped. *Someone's coming! Oh my God someone's coming!* "Please help me!" she uttered, breathing heavily in anticipation.

As the figure moved closer to the bed, she exhaled with relief. "Lainey! Please help me! I just need... that unmm... medicine on the ummm... the... damn it... the little table thing! Just give it to me, *please*... Help me!" Claudia panted.

"Not to get loose... not to escape... not even to hand you the water? Help you get high?"

"You don't under- I need it! *Now*! I'll do *anything*..."

She watched her partner stare down at her like the disgusting mess she was, begging for a fix. She felt so judged but didn't care at that moment. She really just needed to feel the warmth flow through her body, relaxing her horribly tensed and distressed muscles, sending her somewhere exquisite.

"After what you did to me, Claudia, I can't help you. But I'll see you soon."

Her eyes widened as she watched Lainey walk away. "Noooo! Come back!" Claudia shrieked. "What did I doooo..." she cried, watching in shock as Lainey vanished right before her eyes. Though she was too dehydrated to shed tears, Claudia's entire body agonizingly trembled as she wept, realizing that she was hallucinating from the withdrawal and that no one was coming for her.

26

Burgess announced to the room, "We finally got access to the parkway videos!"

Rainer assumed, even though the recordings were outside of their jurisdiction, that would be a much easier task. The parkway cameras and the weather bugs were all accessible to the public online. However, when they went to search the date range they needed, the footage for multiple cameras said, "Unavailable to view." They were told that the cameras had recorded footage, they just weren't able to display every camera online 24/7.

After obtaining a warrant and PennDOT sending over the missing camera recordings, the group was finally able to sift through the hours of footage from the nine cameras that covered the on-ramp closest to Claudia's residence through the Aliquippa exit where Hope's car was dumped.

Captain Higgins stepped out of his office, squeezing his eyes shut with his hands on his hips. "What's that you guys say? 10 out of 10 do not recommend? I'm too damn old for this. I have old eyes!" he complained in response to helping his team sift through video footage. He wanted justice for

Hope and to have Claudia found just as badly as everyone else.

"Ayy. Ayyy! Is this it?" Torrey yelled as the group hustled over.

"Shit yeah! I was right! Look at that!" Burgess gloated, watching the champagne-colored Nissan with a much smaller slate-colored convertible poorly attached to the back.

"That's not the parkway," Rainer observed. "And it's going in the wrong direction from what her phone trace is telling us."

"It's actually the camera at the intersection of Broadhead Road and Kennedy Boulevard," Torrey offered.

"But her phone rode down the parkway all the way to the turnpike. So... it must've been tossed into another vehicle well before when we thought it was."

Torrey pointed out, "The SUV turns onto Mill St., then is out of range because there are no more cameras until you get down to the plaza at the bottom of the hill."

Blowing up the screenshot, they were able to verify the last three digits of Hope's license plate number, but the car attached didn't have one on the back.

"Okay, so he must have removed the plate."

"You guys, who the hell hitches a $100,000 car to the back of a Nissan like that? I would be a nervous wreck!" Rainer noted.

"I would personally be more nervous about the body in the trunk," Burgess hinted.

"Well, there can't be too many people in this city who own a Mercedes-Benz SL-Class convertible," Higgins said as Torrey began to pull the list of registrations.

Eyebrows were raised when Torrey's search revealed 28 owners within a 60-mile radius of Downtown Pittsburgh.

"Seven of them are gray... aaand..." he uttered hesitantly, "Only one belongs to... Dr. Alessandra Berardi."

They all exchanged silent glances, sickened at the thought of how Weston could be involved in this.

Torrey continued clicking through the registration pages until something disturbing caught his eye.

"Guys. I umm... I have a confession," Torrey stammered softly with his eyes to the ground. He jumped when he looked up to see an angry Maceo staring down at him.

"What is it," he angrily growled, fuming at the thought of Weston possibly being involved in hurting Claudia and killing Hope.

Torrey immediately wondered how long he had been behind them watching. They were all so engrossed in the video footage and screen grabs on the large monitor up front that they didn't even notice him enter.

"Talk!"

"James!" Higgins warned, stepping in front of the heated FBI agent.

"I went out to Weston's house last week. He didn't answer, but his Tesla was there. I just figured he was home and hiding out, not wanting any company," Torrey said nervously, glancing up at Maceo. "I peeked into the garage and there was another SUV, but it was covered."

"Who covers a car that's inside of a garage?" Rainer questioned.

"That's exactly what I thought!" Torrey replied. "So uhh... says here that in addition to her Audi SQ8, Alessandra also has registered in her name a black Mercedes-Benz GLE."

The room remained cluelessly silent, awaiting further explanation. This wasn't their case; they didn't have a tech report.

"The paint transfer on Dr. Berardi's Audi was a metallic obsidian black... manufactured by Mercedes-Benz."

"How do you know that?" Higgins inquired.

"Lainey had been following the investigation, I guess. I found it in her notepad," Torrey admitted, picking it up and then tossing it back down onto the desk.

"You stole that from her personal effects?" Higgins accused.

Torrey paused. "Of course not. Penelope gave it to me when I helped her load the car that day she was here."

Rage swelled within Maceo. "You knew that man killed his pregnant wife - *my friend* - all this time, and you ain't say nothin'!?"

"No! I had no idea! I'm *literally* just seeing the car registered to Alessandra right now!"

"James! Calm it... *down*," Higgins ordered, noticing a huffing and enraged Maceo. "Ok let's get a-"

"There's more…" Torrey meekly interjected, glancing back up at a furious Maceo. "I uhhh… I… saw…"

"Spit it out, man!" Mace angrily ordered.

"I saw who I thought was Weston watching you and Claudia in Costco."

"And you ain't *say* shit!? That was *WEEKS* ago! The fuck is wrong wit'chu?" Maceo fired back, forcefully pushing Higgins out of his way so hard that he almost fell over the desk. Snatching Torrey out of his seat, Mace began pummeling him. They both hit the ground as he unleashed all of his fury onto Jonas' face while he tried his best to defend himself. But Jonas was at a disadvantage, as Maceo had more strength and wrath. It took both Higgins and Burgess to peel Maceo from their colleague, while Rainer grabbed Torrey and quickly slid him back out of punching range of the infuriated agent.

"Get the fuck offa me," Maceo growled, shaking his body from their grasp. "We fuckin' *better* find Claudia alive or I will kill you my*self*," Maceo threatened before rampaging out of the precinct.

"Torrey, you are done for the day! Leave!" Higgins loudly ordered. "Burgess, get an emergency warrant for the Grant home and surrounding property, now!" he yelled, running out after Maceo to stop him from going to Weston's house and doing anything rash. Even though he didn't currently work for them, Higgins did not want to risk Maceo busting into that house before they had a warrant and potentially nullifying anything that search would turn up. He knew Maceo wouldn't want that either, but he was clearly loaded for bear and not in his right mind. The man just threatened to kill a detective in a police station, so Higgins had no doubt that if Maceo found Weston, he would absolutely shoot him on site.

27

Angry and embarrassed, Jonas picked himself up off the floor, grabbed his chair that had rolled off in the opposite direction, and sat down at his desk, huffing. He understood the hostility and rage overflowing from Maceo because that's how he felt when Brenna died. Hell, that's how he still felt - like he could fight the world.

He massaged and shifted his throbbing jaw he could feel enlarging by the second. Rainer handed him a baggie of ice wrapped in a paper towel. "Thanks."

"No problem. You ok?"

"Yeah, I will be," Jonas sighed, wincing as he held the ice against his swollen cheek.

As he leaned onto his desk, considering his role in all of this, he couldn't help but think of how Maceo would have reacted had he found out that Jonas actually had a similar plan. Well, one that didn't include murdering Claudia's sister.

Did he want answers that he was convinced she was lying about? Yes. Would he have been willing to hurt her to get them? As angry as he was about losing his fiancée, yes. Did he think he could actually get away with murdering her if it came to it? He did. But maybe that was just his ego and arrogance talking. Then he thought about it... Something he hadn't even considered - had he abducted her to get the answers he wanted, of course, she would tell. So, unless he was prepared to go to jail for the truth, he would've *had* to kill her and make it look like someone or something else happened. At that moment, after Maceo seemingly had knocked some sense into him, he was kind of glad he bitched up, as Penelope called it.

Leaning on his desk, he glanced at the picture in the frame of his birthday bonfire at Claudia's house. Someone had taken a candid photo of the group from atop the small hill at the edge of her gravel driveway. In it, friends were socializing around the fire, Brenna was hugging Jonas, and something he never even noticed before because he was so focused on how cute he and his girl were. Claudia was in the background, off in the cut, staring at Cairo. But then again, the statuesque canine drew eyes constantly. He was stunning, and it was kind of hard not to gawk.

Jonas opened his vehicle's app to start and warm up his car as he began to pack up his belongings to leave. He glanced down to pick up Lainey's small notepad, then looked over to the picture frame. As he focused back on the notepad, he flipped to the next page with the drawing and then slowly rotated the notepad. The picture - Lainey must've just grabbed the notepad and started scribbling not noticing that it was upside down.

What he thought was a giant arrow now looked like a quickly drawn house... those scribbles and random lines off to the right - the bushes and trees that were on the other side of Claudia's lawn? It looked like a way more remedial version of some of the search location diagrams Jana had shown him.

"Holy shit," Jonas muttered, shoving everything into his bag more quickly.

"What's up?" Rainer asked.

"Uh, nothing... See ya tomorrow," Jonas replied, rushing out of the squad room.

"Rainer! Let's roll, little Raven!" Burgess announced, rushing out as well to get the search warrant for Weston's house signed by the judge.

Torrey burst through the doors of his home, greeted by an excited Cairo. "Hey buddy, go get your leash. Let's go!"

By the time Jonas had grabbed a warmer coat for himself and Cairo's stylish new argyle winter coat, he was prancing in anticipatory circles around the leash. As they left the house and headed to the car, Jonas shook his head at the fact that Cairo looked trendier in his winter wear than he did.

As they slowly drove down the windy, desolate road toward Claudia's house, Jonas carefully pulled over. Light and fluffy snowflakes began to fall - the kind that are so airy that they make horrible snowballs, but once accumulated, they're fun to scoop and eat. Despite the chill in the air, Cairo always had his head dangling out the half-open window. As soon as Jonas stopped the car, Cairo began furiously barking.

"Cai!" Jonas yelled.

He got out of the driver's side and walked around to the back passenger side, but before he could attach the leash to Cairo's collar, he immediately pushed through the partially open door and sprinted down the hill.

"Cairo! Shit!" Jonas hissed, running after the eager canine, trying not to slide down the slight but now snowy grade to catch up.

Jonas swallowed, trying to hold back tears when he saw Cairo circle, then lay down near the spot where they found Brenna. His heart hurt listening to Cairo whimper and cry lying as flat as he could to be as close to her as possible. It broke his heart that her dog was grieving as much as he was.

Jonas gave Cairo a few minutes, stroking his head and that spot behind his ears he liked for comfort.

"Ok Cai, we got a job to do here. Let's make Mama proud, Okay? C'mon," he said encouragingly, attaching his leash.

Cairo got up, sniffed around once more, and then walked with Jonas. The plan was to go back to the bottom of the hill and start there, along where the trees lined the open, grassy lot they occupied. But before he could get to the edge to officially start, Cairo pulled to the left and walked, sniffing the ground periodically. Just past two of the trees into the woods, Cairo took a seat and looked to Jonas for approval.

"Good boy, Cairo," he praised, offering him a treat.

He brushed the snow and dead leaves from the area. He knew he probably shouldn't have been touching it and should have immediately called for backup, but the way Cairo so confidently sat down without a second thought, he had to know what, or who was down there. Would they even be recognizable?

The ground was pretty hard due to the low temperatures, so Jonas was having trouble easily moving the earth aside to find out what lay beneath.

"Come," he commanded, jogging back up to his running car and opening the door for Cairo to hop in and warm up. He then browsed his trunk for any sort of tool he could use to loosen the soil.

Returning with a tire iron, Jonas stabbed it not too deep into the ground, just enough to loosen it so that he could use his gloved hands to move the dirt aside. Cairo intently watched from above as he gently and neatly dug, keeping all he'd removed in a small pile in case there was any evidence to be found in it. He dug in the cold weather for what felt like forever when he finally touched something that wasn't supposed to be there.

28

"Higgins" he gruffly answered his ringing cell phone.

"Hey Cap, it's Torrey. Look, I found something you need to-"

"I thought I told you to go home!"

"I was, I did, but," Jonas explained as he attached images of a transparent tarp that clearly contained a human body. All that was visible in the small hole was the side of the head and a portion of the forehead, but the victim appeared to be a Black male. "I got a hunch from Lainey's notepad, so I came out here."

"Oh my Gah," Higgins replied as the images came through one by one. "Where the hell is '*here?*'"

"Um... On the outer edge of Claudia's property," he responded, looking around nervously.

Higgins' heart nearly stopped. "Okay ummm," he stammered, still shocked. "I'm going to send the forensic team and get a warrant for her residence and property as well. Stay with the body, I'm sending Rainer over so one of you can wait at the house until the warrant is secured. We're all still here at the Grant residence."

"Anything turn up?"

"Not yet. Not sure how long ago, but he definitely blew town. The kids' personal items are gone. We're putting out a BOLO for him and both his and Dr. Berardi's vehicles. Also looping in the FBI and Interpol because he absolutely has the means to flee the country."

"Rainer!" Higgins yelled, abruptly ending the call. "Get the keys from Burgess and head over to Martinez's place. He can ride back with me. Torrey found a body."

"It's not Claudia, is it?"

"No. Thankfully. Get out there now! He'll fill you in. Take this."

"Yes, Captain," Rainer said, hustling to follow his instructions.

"Director Yeager! Higgins here..."

As she pulled up behind Torrey's running car, Rainer spotted Cairo inside. She gave him some love through the open window before heading down the hill.

"Oh damn," Rainer mumbled, peeking into the shallow hole. "Captain had me bring this tarp," she said, removing it from the plastic. "It doesn't seem like we need it under these dense pine-looking trees. There's no snow falling here, but I guess, throw it over anyway?"

He helped her open and place the tarp over the area so no additional contamination would occur.

"If you wanna wait in your car here, I'll head up and wait at her house."

Rainer nodded.

Jonas was still in shock behind all of this. He needed to talk it out and Cairo was an excellent listener. "So, did Lainey find this body and that's why Claudia shot her? She claims Lainey shot her first, but maybe that's not what happened? Could Lainey and Brenna have been down there looking for that body and she just shot them both? Maybe Lainey's bullet was the one in self-defense? I wonder who it is."

Cairo sat, gazing into Jonas' eyes as though he could understand the conversation. He then rested his head on Jonas' shoulder.

"Good boy, Cai," he praised, generously giving him ear scratches. "So glad Mama didn't take you down there with her."

He stood behind a pillar in sunglasses and clothing that made him queasy but look completely unrecognizable as a valid Pittsburgher - a Cincinnati Bengals tee and matching ball cap. This was squarely against his sports religion, but the now dirty blond-haired man with a clean-shaven face needed to do what he had to do.

Human memory is a funny thing. People are more likely to look at and readily recall the giant tiger on the front of his shirt than his facial features from under that cap.

With his head low, he punched in all the numbers individually, then patiently waited for the text to send.

Det. Jonas Torrey; Det. Eric Burgess; Capt. Edward Higgins; Dir. Anthony Yeager; IA Bradley Pitt; DA Jason Lind; ADA Sherring Hill; ME Kathryn Hale; and most importantly Agent Maceo James. They would all eventually open their phones to a riveting attachment from Weston, with a simple text that read, "I left the light on for you."

Upon receiving confirmation, he immediately powered off the burner cell phone, removed the SIM card along with his prints from the phone, and discreetly tossed it into the trash before boarding his next flight from Switzerland to Montenegro.

Cairo's heavy head popped up when Jonas' phone loudly vibrated. He glanced down at it, immediately annoyed that someone would have added him to a group chat. Those were the worst because the constant notifications usually annoyed everyone in the group.

Jonas was confused at first. "Left the light on... Ain't no damn Motel 6. What's that even mean?" The attachment he clicked on was dark, and he didn't know what he was looking at beyond the flashing red and blue police lights brightly illuminating his screen. He flinched and gasped at the quiet sound of the two gunshots through the silencer.

With wide eyes, Jonas watched the shooter collect the two shell casings from the ground and rifle through the victim's car. As the shooter slowly turned to walk away from the car, the amateur filmmaker shakily zoomed in to reveal the face of Detective Claudia Martinez.

"Holy shit!"

29

Jonas stuffed his phone into his pocket, immediately jumped out of the car, and sprinted to Claudia's front door, glancing up at the illuminated porch light that he hadn't noticed since it was still daylight.

He stared at the shiny doorknob thinking, *it can't be this easy. She can't have been out here in her own house the whole time.* He slowly lifted his hand to the knob and turned it until the door squeaked open. The house was dark and almost as cold inside as it was outside.

Jonas drew his weapon and slowly walked down the entryway toward the open main living space. He cleared that room before proceeding straight through and down the hall. He tapped open each door to make sure each room was clear and continued to the end of the corridor toward the closed door.

Jonas' heart pulsed heavily in his chest not knowing what he was going to find behind that door. He twisted the knob to slowly open it to find total darkness, unlike the other rooms that were lit by natural light coming through the windows. The raw sewage-like odor hit him before anything else.

He pulled his coat collar up over his nose and then panned his cell phone flashlight across the room until he gasped in horror. In all his years on the force, he hadn't ever seen anything quite this disturbing. Claudia's delicate body, covered in bruises and dried blood, one arm and the opposite leg restrained to her bed, lying in her own filth. Locating then sliding on the light, with his gun still in hand, he made his way over to the master bathroom and opened the door to the walk-in closet to be sure they were all clear, then carefully made his way over to the bed. The smell of old blood and vomit in front of the busted-up nightstand didn't mix well with the fecal odor coming from Claudia's bed. His first thought was to open a window, but that's when he noticed they were all boarded up.

Jonas knew he should have immediately called it in. But she already looked deceased, and if she wasn't, part of him wanted her to be, which meant the sooner he alerted people to her presence here, the more likely she would be to get help and would end up at the desk beside him - again! Not only had she shot his fiancée and two of his colleagues, but he also just watched a video of her murdering an innocent man. And let's not forget the body buried in the backyard. In his mind, she didn't deserve help.

Through the sheer, yellow, babydoll nightie, Jonas could see all the damage done to her now frail, naked body, including the still-healing but visibly infected "W" branded into her upper inner thigh. As the first one on the scene, he knew he had to be the one to verify if she was, in fact, alive or not.

Walking around to the other side of the bed, he reached for her outstretched arm, then jumped when she slowly opened her eyes and looked not as much at him, but through him.

"Claudia!" he panted heavily. The condition she was in, he was honestly shocked she was still alive!

Her eyes focused on him before looking away. He was just another hallucination. Everyone who came to the room was. No one would help her get her "medicine." He wouldn't either.

"This is Detective Jonas Torrey. I have an officer down and need a medic at 14205 Hollow Lane Dr."

Then he switched off his radio.

"You're... real?" she barely uttered through cracked, peeling, dry lips.

"Yes," he replied, walking back over for the bottle on her nightstand. He knew he likely wouldn't get answers from her in this condition, but that wasn't going to stop him from trying.

She gasped as she greedily and desperately sucked down the water, even looking forward to the bitter taste. But it didn't have one. It seemed to be normal water.

Though the worst of the withdrawal symptoms had passed, if she could just get to her medicine, everything would be better.

"Can you... untie..."

"I can't. But someone will be here soon with the bolt cutter," he lied, staring at the key to the handcuffs on the nightstand.

"My... medicine... Can I- *please*?" she begged.

"Claudia, who did this to you?" he asked for verification, ignoring her request.

"Where... is he?" she panted, fearfully shifting her eyes around the room as though she were waiting for him to jump out and assault her again.

"Who is *he*?"

She paused, afraid to say his name. "Weston," she eventually whispered, her jaw still unable to move properly. "My... medicine..."

"Do you know *why* he did this to you?"

She slowly shook her aching head no.

"Seriously!?" he questioned, trying so hard to keep the anger out of his voice.

"I just... woke... up like... this," she whimpered.

"You're not fucking Beyoncé," Jonas hissed, failing at his initial effort to maintain control of himself.

Claudia's breathing began to shift, nervous that he was going to start beating her too. From her vantage, Torrey looked and sounded how Weston did before his rage exploded. Why was everyone so angry at her?

"Please... What do you... think... I did?"

Jonas glared down at her to see true confusion and terror in her eyes. "Do you seriously not remember all the people you murdered?"

"What? No... I- I help..."

"You *shot* Tanner," he interrupted.

"I-" she shifted her eyes, struggling to remember anything.

"You *killed* Lainey."

"Noo- I-" With her eyes squeezed shut, her heart rate quickened, causing her breathing to shallow. "Not Lainey. I could never-"

"And you *murdered* my fiancée, Brenna," Jonas growled in a dark tone.

Claudia's breathing stopped, before slowly exhaling, shaking her head no. She wasn't a murderer. She would never intentionally hurt anyone. "I... don't... *I couldn't...*"

It was only when she turned her head and gazed longingly at the nightstand that he realized Weston had her completely strung out. She was going through withdrawal. Was that why she was struggling to remember? Or was she just playing dumb? Was this supposed to be a set-up for her defense in court? He would never be able to forgive himself if that were the case, and she got off for all this shit.

He walked over to the nightstand and asked, "Is this your *medicine*?"

She nodded desperately, beginning to breathe more heavily and twitching in anticipation.

"*Please...*"

That syringe was full to the brim. There was no way that she could survive being injected with that much of anything.

He stood, heavily considering his options. If he injected her, there would be a new mark, and he was the last one with her. They knew Weston had been gone, so the last track mark would have been from a few days ago. He had already called it in, so without knowing what exactly was in the syringe, he theoretically could inject her, only for it to take too long to kill her, then they show up and still save her worthless life.

As he listened to her desperately beg him, he then wondered if it would be more of a punishment to not give it to her. But the thought of her showing up to work in six months, taking a seat beside him like nothing fucking happened, quite literally enraged him to the brink of tears.

Both breathing heavily for different reasons, Jonas tightened the tie that was already around her upper arm. He could hear memories of Brenna and all his deceased friends in his head as he slowly removed the cap, waiting for a vein to enlarge.

"I can't let you hurt anyone else," he cried as he made the decision to inject her in a spot that wouldn't be noticeable - her already open and bleeding wrist near the handcuff, praying he got the vein. She was so dehydrated, that none were visible, even with the tourniquet.

He watched her body gyrate with anticipation, mildly annoyed that he would be putting her out of her misery but grateful that he would never have to see her again.

As he inserted the needle into her anxiously awaiting wrist, Jonas heard multiple footsteps and commotion thundering down the hallway toward the bedroom.

"Fuck!"

Jonas jumped away after sliding the syringe back onto the nightstand just before the paramedics burst through the door, immediately tending to Claudia. They were followed by Higgins and Burgess.

"Ohhh my gah," Higgins painfully faltered when he saw the condition his detective was in. He looked around the room and then at Torrey. "Why didn't you uncuff her?"

"I was waiting for someone to come with the bolt cutter."

"The key is on the fucking nightstand!!" he yelled.

Carefully avoiding the blood and vomit on the floor, Higgins handed the one paramedic the key as the other searched diligently for a vein to begin to administer I.V. fluids to the severely dehydrated woman.

Higgins looked on as an angry, combative Claudia yelled as best she could, swearing and glaring at Jonas for not giving her the medicine he promised! They ended up having to sedate her so they could insert a central line in her chest.

The captain narrowed his eyes at Torrey, who then felt the need to explain.

"She kept asking for her medicine, but I told her that I couldn't and that help would be here in a few minutes."

"Hmmm... Medicine... Are you referring to the syringe that's right beside the handcuff key?"

They stared at one another as Jonas tried to control his breathing.

Maceo came barreling through the house, physically halted by Burgess and Higgins.

"Hey! No! You don't wanna see her like-" But both of them combined were no match for his desperation to make sure his girl was okay. He pushed through their blockade like a bear on steroids rushing into her master bedroom.

He became light-headed, and the entire room shook when he saw her condition. He almost vomited himself at the thought of what Weston could have done to have her in that condition in only two weeks. Maceo teared up, watching as the paramedics worked on her until Higgins and Burgess approached.

"I told you that you didn't want to see her. Let them work. She's alive. That's what matters. Come on," Higgins consoled, slowly backing him out of the room.

30

There was no one else to speak to. Claudia's only next of kin had been murdered and her parents had passed away years ago. As her stepmother, Ms. Emma was who the physicians were authorized to speak to, but really, it was Maceo who was the closest to her. Mace could barely hold himself together as the doctor discussed with them everything that had happened to her, from the starvation to the drug addiction to the sexual assault and battery to the brand permanently emblazoned into the tender flesh of her upper, inner thigh.

Plastic surgeons had the grand undertaking of repairing her broken nose and performing reconstructive surgery on pretty much the entire right side of Claudia's face. Because her jaw had been fractured in several places, they had to repair and wire it shut, so she would be unable to speak once she awakened. There was a feeding tube in place to provide the missing nutrients, and an I.V. delivering fluids and antibiotics, in addition to pain meds. Surgeons also had to repair the work already done on her shoulder that had sustained the initial gunshot injury. She had already gone through withdrawal cold turkey once, so they elected to sedate her for the next five days so her body could heal.

Was she under arrest? Absolutely. Did the public know yet? No. Because the only evidence tying her to the murder of Jerry Marcuse was the video, of course, the people who had received it were not releasing it to the media. It would be held close to the vest until they verified the validity of it.

Under normal circumstances, when an arrested patient is hospitalized, they would be restrained to the bed. But because of everything she had just endured, waking up again physically restricted would be even more traumatic. So, Claudia was fitted with an ankle monitor, and an officer was stationed outside of her hospital room 24/7. Doctors and nurses simply thought it was for her protection and were none the wiser that she was suspected of murdering the two men found in their cars, in addition to her possible involvement in the murder of Levar. She had been cleared of any charges surrounding Lainey's shooting because it was deemed self-defense, but she hadn't yet been cleared of charges in the accidental death of Brenna.

Days later, Claudia awakened in a room that wasn't hers. That was a good thing. But she could hear the beeps from the monitor as her heart rate drastically increased when she set her eyes on the stranger in the chair beside her bed, with his upper body leaned onto it, soundly sleeping. The sturdy hand she felt on her leg caused her to lash out in fear as all the memories of what had happened flooded back.

"Claudia, it's ok!" Mace tried to soothe her, but she was inconsolable, grunting and shaking. She tried to scream out but realized she couldn't even open her mouth.

A nurse pushed past the uniformed officer outside of her hospital room.

"Claudia... Claudia..." the nurse calmly spoke, holding her hand and letting her know she was okay and that she was safe. "My name is Olivia, and I'm your nurse today. Can you slow your breathing for me?" she asked, gently inhaling with her until she calmed down. "I'm going to grab the doctor, okay?"

As she tried to leave, Claudia's breathing picked up again as she held tightly onto her hand, staring wide-eyed in fear at the stranger dripping with concern at the foot of her bed.

"Claudia, it's ok. It's Maceo," the nurse nodded.

Olivia spoke so confidently because that man had not left her bedside for the week since she had been admitted.

But Olivia's proclamations about her safety did nothing to assuage Claudia's fear and anxiety. She would not release Olivia's hand.

"You don't remember Maceo?" she asked.

Claudia frantically shook her head no, still breathing heavily. Though she did vaguely remember Weston mentioning that name while brutally assaulting her. And every time that name crossed his lips, the rage and brutality seemed to heighten. In her mind, she associated

Maceo with much of the physical agony she had endured and began hyperventilating again.

"Claudia, *baby*... It's *me*. It's *Mace*," he said, broken-hearted that she was so fearful and didn't seem to remember him.

"Sir, I'm sorry but I'm going to have to ask you to leave," Olivia demanded, pressing the button to summon other nurses in to help sedate Claudia once again.

31

Weeks passed with Claudia still in the hospital, having been moved from a regular room to the psych unit where she could still receive medical care and physical rehab but remain on lockdown.

Even though her jaw had completely healed, and she was back to eating regular foods, she still hadn't spoken. Not a single word since Higgins had shown her the text Weston sent. It was like seeing a ghost. She watched herself murder that man, cover her tracks, and leave like nothing had ever happened. Then, to find out that there was another victim matching that MO, which meant more than likely it was her, might have stunned her into silence. The worst part was that she had absolutely no recollection of any of it. She could never imagine herself taking a life unnecessarily. But there she was in the proverbial flesh in a video that was thoroughly examined and deemed authentic.

Then, to also learn that the body they found on her property belonged to Levar? Sweet, goofy coffee shop Levar. Yes, the body was on her property, but so was Lainey, who had already allegedly murdered and dismembered a number of people. Claudia's attorney suggested that Lainey could've murdered Levar and left the body on Claudia's property to frame her just as she had done to Tanner.

The problem was, however, that they found very well-hidden wallets, jewelry, and watches belonging to Dan Hogan and Jerry Marcuse on her property. That, combined with the video of her shooting one of them, was a slam dunk for the prosecution. What further complicated things was when Rainer's investigation into those two victims revealed the wayward similarities to many of the victims who had been eliminated by "the Keeper." This led prosecutor Sherring Hill to believe that Claudia was somehow working with Lainey and Tanner - a team of law enforcement officers showing up to crime scenes to solve crimes that *they* had committed. With that video out, Claudia had no choice but to admit that she had done it but, against recommendations, demanded to plead not guilty by reason of mental disease or defect. That was not a defense that attorneys liked to use because proving it can be a nightmare, and Claudia's excuse of *I just didn't remember*, was not going to make it any easier.

ADA Sherring Hill was not buying any of it and refused the defense's plea agreement to send her to the state mental hospital. She sought to prove the detective was faking the memory loss to avoid the death penalty, so she requested a jury trial.

That didn't bode well for her when the prosecution called Dr. Sydney Pearce to the stand, not to testify about

Claudia's mental health but to testify about being Claudia's only surviving victim.

Though she was unable to clearly verbalize the events of that night due to her traumatic brain injury, she was able to testify via an electronic communication device. Claudia teared up as she, the jury, her former colleagues, and of course, Maceo listened in revulsion to her beloved therapist share the story of coming home and finding who she *thought* was Claudia in her house. It was only when she threatened to send her daughter Crystal back to her in pieces that she realized the woman sitting across from her was responsible for many, if not *all*, of the murders.

On cross-examination, Claudia's defense attorney questioned why Dr. Pearce kept referring to Claudia as "that woman."

The banging of the gavel, along with the judge hollering "Order in the court!" was all that could be heard after Dr. Pearce answered that Claudia was a kind soul who she didn't think would ever hurt anyone and that the woman who shot her wasn't Claudia. "She said her name was Ruby."

Maceo sat stunned in the courtroom, realizing that all that time he had been in a relationship with Ruby and not Claudia. That's why she didn't remember him. He legitimately wasn't sure how to feel about any of it. He was in love with that woman, and yes, she killed those men, but it wasn't without reason. As crazy as it sounded, she saved lives. The only reason he could figure Dr. Pearce ended up on the list was because she was astute enough to figure it out and was deemed a threat by Ruby.

When the prosecution asked to redirect, ADA Hill questioned why she didn't say anything or report that she suspected such. But it was only that morning in Claudia's appointment that Dr. Pearce had truly begun to suspect a dissociative identity disorder diagnosis. She hadn't even gotten another appointment with Claudia to be able to delve more into her suspicions. It would be reckless to just make a snap diagnosis of that magnitude without additional discussion and confirmation.

To further validate Dr. Pearce's claims that Claudia was not the person who had shot her, the defense subpoenaed the audio interviews that internal affairs had conducted with Detective Martinez's colleagues. Every single one of them initially told IA that "Claudia in a million years would never intentionally hurt anyone."

But that didn't mean that Ruby wouldn't. Dr. Pearce could see that Claudia was *currently* Claudia. But there was no way to ensure that she *stayed* Claudia. Trauma was what brought Ruby out in the first place, maybe that's what put her back into hibernation, so to speak? Maybe she just wasn't strong enough to stay out once Weston began drugging her? There was no way to know. But she needed specialized help that she would not otherwise receive if she were just thrown into the general population of some women's prison. The jury agreed and found her not guilty by reason of mental disease or defect, which meant she would be sentenced to the psychiatric facility that was housed within the women's prison.

32

Claudia had been placed in one of the state mental hospitals until space opened in the prison's psychiatric unit. She was allowed to have visitors, just as she would if she were incarcerated. So, Maceo stopped by several times. He would talk to her, but she never spoke back. She still hadn't spoken a single word since she was rescued. They also had her on a sedative to keep her in a docile state. So, she just curiously observed the FBI agent and wondered why he would want to even occupy space with her after learning of the heinous things she had done. She was told that they had been in a relationship for the past several months, which blew her mind that she was intimately involved with such a fine and seemingly good man and had absolutely no recollection. Then she wondered how such a good person could have loved her so much as Ruby.

Before departing, Maceo just stared at Claudia. She literally looked like a completely different person to him. Well, because she was. Her appearance was in direct contrast to Ruby's typically sharp, squinted eyes and devilish grin.

Claudia was escorted to an office and seated on the couch. The therapist entered directly behind and picked up her file, flipping through it.

"Detective Claudia... Martinez." Her heart thudded heavily in her chest when she realized that she was, in some form, sitting across from *the Keeper*.

Claudia watched the therapist with concern, noting the immediate difference in her demeanor. Was everyone just going to be afraid of her forever? She didn't do anything wrong.

Setting down the files and observing Claudia for a few moments, she said, "Look, I'm supposed to give you these meds. But I'm not going to. They're only going to make you lethargic and have a host of other horrible side effects. Here. Drink this bottle of water. It'll help you feel better."

Claudia began to breathe heavily as anxiety formed in the pit of her stomach at simply being offered a bottle of water. Weston had said the same thing before drugging her.

"It's ok, Claudia. It's a new bottle. It's sealed," she offered, knowing the details of her abduction.

She stared at the woman suspiciously as she calmed down, cautiously opened the bottle, and began to drink.

Sitting down at her desk, she hit the button for the intercom on her phone to call an orderly.

"Yes ma'am," the muffled voice boomed through the intercom.

"Please come to my office."

Claudia was nervous, wondering why she was being sent away after this woman merely looked at her file.

"What's up, Dr. Reed?"

"Please escort this patient back to her room."

"But it's not-"

"*Now*, please."

"Alrighty... But she can't take the bottle."

They both stared at her, and the therapist nodded supportively. She wasn't sure why, but for some reason, she trusted her, so she immediately chugged down the remainder of the water and handed it to the orderly, who tossed it into the recycle bin.

"Actually, instead, take her out to the terrace. She's not feeling well, and some fresh air may be more therapeutic for her than anything we could accomplish here since she's still not talking."

After an hour on the terrace trying to figure out what the hell just happened back there, the orderly escorted Claudia back to her room.

That evening, other than lying in the uncomfortable bed curled into a fetal position, she felt good. This was the longest she had been without some form of sedative in her system in what felt like ages. Weston kept her drugged, the hospital had her on pain meds, then after that, she was constantly being forced some sort of sedative because everyone was so worried about Ruby coming out to play.

With her back to the door, Claudia heard the beep from someone using a badge to access her room. She turned to find the therapist from earlier.

"Detective," she whispered, standing at the wall. "I have something for you," she alluded, pulling a flat item from under the back of her sweater, setting it down beside her on the bed, and then stepping back. "And here's this too. I've had it for years, so they won't be able to trace the purchase back to me, and definitely not to you."

She handed the phone to Claudia who deliberately looked around the room suspiciously. She instantly thought this was a setup in some way to entrap her so they would have a reason to lock her away in the basement of some maximum-security prison.

She slowly reached out toward the woman offering her the means of communication. But before she touched it, she quietly uttered, "This- this is a trap," using her scratchy, wavering voice for the first time in months. "You're trying to trick me."

"No!" she assured, shaking her head with sincere eyes.

"Um... My name is Rebecca Reed, but you may remember me as R. My husband was Charlie Reed."

Claudia was so confused because she didn't know a Rebecca or a Charlie.

"Or... I guess maybe you don't remember. But you helped me out of a really shitty situation, and you probably saved my daughter Josie's life. There's no way I could ever repay you for that. None of us can. But this is the least *I* can do. You are needed, and I'm certain there is no shortage of people who'd be willing to help you like you've helped us. The shifts will change at midnight," she said, nodding her head, then exiting the room without locking the door.

Claudia stared down in total disbelief at the unopened pack of lavender scrubs, a mask, a small wad of cash, and a key card sitting at the foot of her bed. Could it really be that simple? All she had to do was put on the scrubs and mask and exit the building with the rest of the employees.

I can't do this, she thought to herself nervously as her breathing shifted. *I can't just leave. Where would I even go? I have no money. They would find me. This is crazy!*

Her mind continued frantically reeling, eyes shifting desperately around the room as she began hyperventilating. *My sister is dead. Every friend I have is in law enforcement. Like, there's literally nowhere for me to go! Why would that woman... I can't do this! This is insane! I can't...* Her body began to gradually calm itself and she inhaled deeply, then stretched her stiffened neck. "Simple bitch..." Ruby talked to her inner self as she promptly tore off her clothes and slid into the scrubs. "I *thought* you would be able to get through to Weston better than I could. That clearly didn't fucking work. I *definitely* knew you could sway any jury with those enormous, innocent eyes better than I could. I'm aware of my shortcomings. But *this* ain't one of them." She stuffed the cash and the phone into her pocket, waited for the appropriate time, and casually exited the building with the other employees. Her very first stop would be to pay a visit to Detective Jonas Torry. *That little idiot was actually gonna kill me.*

Maceo was curled up on his couch watching a movie on the theater-size screen he called a television when he received a text message from an unknown number that simply read, *River-walk under the bridge. Come now.*

He frowned in bewilderment, excused himself, and then threw on a pair of shoes.

"Where are you going?" the female voice questioned.

"I'll be right back," he said, quickly exiting the apartment.

Through his panoramic window, she watched him pull his hoodie up over his head and scurry down the street, until he stopped and looked around at the water's edge. Wondering why he'd be under a bridge at this late hour, she immediately threw pants and shoes on as well.

As Maceo crept past a few of the city's unhoused, a shadowy, hooded figure emerged from behind the bridge's pillar and approached him, sliding off the hood of the coat she'd stolen from the hospital.

"Claudia!?" he questioned in utter shock.

She didn't reply. She simply stared dangerously but longingly into his eyes.

"Ruby..." he gasped, quickly closing the distance between them. "What? How did you..."

"I know I shouldn't be here," she interrupted. "But I needed to see you once more before I go."

Mace reached for and held her hand. He hadn't touched her in *so* long.

"I know a guy who does exceptional passport work and he-"

"Ruby, you know they're not lettin' you get anywhere near an airplane, right? Your face is gon' be all over the news by morning."

"That's why I have to leave tonight."

"Where?"

She eyed him skeptically, "You wanna know so you can tell your people where to find me?"

He rushed in and kissed her passionately, their bodies pressed tightly together. "Absolutely not," he assured, resting his forehead against hers, never wanting to let her go, but knowing he had to.

She believed him. "I'm going to find Weston. I believe he's in Monteneg-"

"Baby is everything... ok?" the woman inquired, rushing around the corner and halting in surprise to find Maceo tenderly standing in the arms of another.

"*Baby?*" Ruby questioned skeptically. "Hmmm..." she hissed, sliding her hand from his. "I mean, it's been over a year, so I figured you'd eventually move on, but to my partner?" she said, shooting daggers at the striking ebony woman.

"It's not even like that, we're just... hangin' out," Mace tried to explain.

Detective Denise Rainer ignored Maceo's dismissive statement, more focused on Claudia who was supposed to be securely locked away until the prison system found acid strong enough to dissolve the key.

"Maceo!" she screeched. "Are you fucking *kidding* me!?" She immediately took her phone from her pocket to call it in.

"Denise, No!" Mace yelled.

With her full force and lightning speed, Ruby elbowed Maceo in the throat and pushed past him to physically stop her from making that call. Whipping her around and slamming her against the metal pillar, knocking the air out of her body, then throwing her to the concrete, the phone flew out of Denise's hand. The call connected just as it slid across the ground, stopping inches from falling over the edge into the water.

While still trying to catch his breath, Maceo struggled to pull Ruby off Denise, but she had both fists full of her long, thick natural hair, ferociously smashing her head into the ground.

Maceo was finally able to peel the fuming Ruby from Denise's severely injured body. It was as though time slowed down when Ruby turned toward him and he stared painfully into the deep eyes of the merciless woman he loved, hearing the police sirens in the background growing louder and closer. Visually taking in her loose curls blowing across her impeccable face, illuminated by the red and blue flashing lights rapidly approaching, he knew he needed to arrest her. As much as he wanted to, there was no way he could justify letting her go.

"Ruby, I-" His breathing stopped, and his eyes widened when the bullet from Denise's large caliber gun fired, searing straight through Ruby's core and lodging into

Maceo's behind her. She fell forward into Mace who fell backward, landing at the edge of the river-walk. The phone with the active 9-1-1 call fell into the water and Ruby right after, but Maceo caught her. Struggling for breath and critically injured himself, he clung tightly to Ruby's arm, trying to pull her back up out of the frigid, fast-flowing Allegheny River. But the soaked clothes and shoes weighed her down even more. He was bleeding out, but still striving to hold on to her until the police could make it to them and help.

Denise slowly lost consciousness to the sound of Maceo's distressed cries.

The next morning

Thank you for joining KDKA Pittsburgh Morning News. Search helicopters along with the dive team are scouring the Allegheny and Ohio Rivers in search of the body of former Pittsburgh PD Detective Claudia Martinez. We're told she was shot at the river's edge and her body fell into the water after what appeared to be a confrontation with two other law enforcement officials. Martinez escaped from the psychiatric facility where she was being held while awaiting sentencing for the murders of Dan Hogan and Jerry Marcuse. The other two officers involved in the dispute, Detective Denise Rainer and FBI Agent Maceo James were transported to the hospital in serious condition.

"Bae, did you hear that?" Tanisha asked her husband. "Not this crazy bitch escaping from the nut house!? Seriously!?"

He shook his head, continuing to eat his toast.

We also have breaking news regarding the murder of an off-duty Pittsburgh PD Detective. Jonas Torrey was found stabbed four times outside his home last night and died en route to the hospital. A neighbor told us that 911 was called when his typically well-behaved dog would not stop barking. Stay tuned for more exclusive details as the investigation continues.

"I'm so glad we live out here far away from all the insanity in town. We don't need them problems. Ooh, babe! The contractors are here! Come on!" she announced excitedly.

After speaking to the crew, the couple retreated into the home to get away from the noise.

The trees in the area had already been cleared. "They want the deep end of the pool farthest away from the house," the foreman ordered. "It's marked."

"Got it," the heavy equipment technician replied, putting on his headphones before getting comfortable in the large excavator.

As he rocked out to whatever music was blaring through his earbuds placed inside his noise-canceling protective headphones, he began digging and lifting large amounts of soil, rocks, and tree roots to discard along the side of the rectangular hole that was about to take shape.

He dug and dropped several times until he noticed his boss waving to him. So, he smiled, waved back, and kept on digging and dropping. Unbeknownst to him, every few feet of shifting and scooping the earth, a body would come tumbling out of the bucket and roll clumsily down the mound of dirt.

He eventually realized his boss wasn't waving at him but yelling for him to stop. The operator immediately removed the headphones and looked around. The cigarette he was smoking fell out of his mouth when his jaw dropped open.

The foreman rapped on the sliding glass door. "Mr. and Mrs. Stewart, we have a little problem out back."

As they stepped out, their 9-year-old son squeezed between them, making it to the edge of the deck first. "Ohhhh man! Sooo cool!" he exclaimed, whipping out his phone to take a video. His father immediately pulled it from his hands, stuck it in his pocket, and told his son to go back in the house.

"Awwww, Daaaad, I never get to have any fun!" he grumbled, stomping back inside, but peering excitedly through the window.

As the Stewarts examined the construction site from the deck, they were outraged by what appeared to be three bodies in various stages of decomposition, covered in dirt, each missing a limb.

"I've never seen anything like this. The police have already been notified," the foreman stated.

Within hours, officers, detectives, and a human remains detection dog were on site and had placed eleven other yellow notification flags into the ground indicating the areas to dig for additional remains.

As night fell and Tanisha peeked through the window of the sliding glass door, she found her yard illuminated by bright, portable lights and news crews reporting on techs still digging up bodies from their property. Frustrated, she immediately stormed off.

"Nish, where you going?"

"To call the realtor! Where do you think!?"

"Are you serious? We *literally* just unpacked the last box yesterday."

"And *today* they are unpacking *people* from our *yard*! She sold us *the damn Piece Keeper's* house, Jason! That chick buried folks in the backyard like she was planting daisies! I feel like *this* falls under the category of "shit the realtor needs to disclose!"

"I mean, I'm sure she didn't know about *that* part."

"That is *so* beside the point right now," she hissed while scrolling through her contacts.

The number you are trying to reach is no longer in service...

Bonus Chapter

seven months later...

The elated sounds of children laughing and waves lapping along the shoreline of the ancient yet bustling town of Budva, Montenegro, made for a relaxing, ambient backdrop to the park by the bay. An elderly, grizzled man carefully grasped the armrest as he eased his weight down onto the chipped-green wooden bench, mindful of his bad knees. As he watched his young granddaughter excitedly dart off toward the weatherworn but charming jungle gym, he noticed in his periphery an attractive young lady seated next to him. She seemed deeply preoccupied with a journal she was studiously scribbling in until she heard a throat suddenly being cleared in her general direction. That the exquisite and pleasantly exotic-statured young woman was a tourist was immediately obvious. He grinned and asked in a thick accent, "Visiting for work or pleasure, Miss?"

Her responding smile was dazzling as she tucked a lock of shoulder-length, glossy auburn hair behind her ear and closed her notebook. "Oh, definitely pleasure," she answered amiably. "Guess my disguise for blending in with the locals didn't go as planned. Tell me, what gave me away?"

The older native snickered, "Well, the visitors are usually taking pictures or finding inspiration from the beautiful scenery all around to write their great novels someday." He jovially gestured to her notebook.

"Guilty," the charming woman admitted playfully.

"How lovely. And what is it you do for work?" he asked.

She hesitated for a moment, inhaling deeply, "Let's just say I'm very good at finding things," she answered boldly with a smirk as she turned her darkening gaze, hidden by opaque sunglasses, toward the children romping and shouting.

His granddaughter was now taking turns playing tag with a pair of dark-haired boys who were chasing each other around the swing set. A chiseled, clean-shaven, blond-haired man walked over to round up the twins as he collected their belongings and prepared for them to leave.

"Well, it was nice to meet you. I'd better be off. Lots to do," she remarked eagerly, not taking her eyes off those boys.

"Da, Miss. I hope you enjoy your stay. Any particular plans?"

"Well, between us, there is a special friend I've come to visit. He doesn't know I'm here yet, but he will very soon," she winked mischievously.

"How nice, he will love the surprise, I am sure," the old man beamed.

"Oh, he's going to just *die* when he sees me," she offered with a warm smile.

The old man waved and refocused on his little one playing on the slide as the woman gracefully blended in with the crowd, walking in the same direction Weston had just gone with his identical sons.

Hmm, she thought. *A novel, huh? Maybe that's not such a bad idea someday after I... retire. I could call it... Confessions of a Sane Single Woman? I wonder if Oprah would read it.*

FBI Director Anthony Yeager nodded as he passed the mail clerk who'd just dropped off some packages, strewn carelessly onto his desk. He began opening them one by one until a knock on his door interrupted him.

"You wanted to see me?" Maceo asked, stepping into the office.

"Yes. Close the door. I need an update on the Colter trafficking case."

As Maceo began informing the director, he continued opening the packages, nodding as he listened. He sliced through the tape on the square cardboard box to find a white Styrofoam container with a typed note on top that simply read, *the Keeper is still watching.*

His grimaced face made Maceo slow down his update, then eventually stop to approach the desk.

With a frown, Yeager immediately set the note down, grabbed a pair of latex gloves, and then shimmied up the lid. Maceo looked on nervously as Yeager continued to unwrap layer upon layer of chilled bubble wrap until he revealed a red box with a matching bow. His mouth dropped when Yeager opened it to find the miniature box full. "Are those… teeth? Those are *teeth!* And *fingernails!?*" Maceo exclaimed, jumping back.

Yeager continued digging deeper into the chilled container to uncover a decomposing left hand donning a platinum wedding band. It was holding a disposable cell phone encased in a clear baggie. Yeager removed it and powered it on to find a message on the home screen. *You have no idea how much it arouses me to return the favor. Since your friend here likes sending videos so much, press play.*

The two watched in repulsion as *every* gruesome thing that had been done to Claudia was *repeatedly* done to Weston. She sent *weeks* of daily footage which included everything from her removing teeth with a rusty pair of pliers to him wailing in agony as she branded all *three* of her initials into the underside of his-

"I'm gonna be sick," Yeager uttered, slamming the flip phone closed, diligently trying to hold down his lunch. His entire body shuddered when the phone in his hand violently vibrated.

Hearts racing, the two men stared at each other in abject horror as Yeager slowly opened the phone to a message that read, *Don't worry, I left your agent alive… Oh, and I left the light on for you too ;)*

"Fuck!" Yeager yelled, sickened at the thought. "Weston's still alive? Left to suffer and starve to death!?" He frantically examined the box to find anything to indicate a location.

Maceo stood calmly watching him. "But that's what he'd planned to do to Claudia. He raped and branded the woman I loved... got her strung out and left her there to *die* all because his fragile little ego couldn't deal with rejection."

Yeager gradually looked up at Maceo, concerned by his serene demeanor in this gruesome moment. With disgust contorting his face, he asked slowly, "Agent James. You know where she's at, don't you?"

Maceo turned his mouth down and shook his head, "Nah... sorry."

He could hear his director shouting his name, demanding that he return as he casually strolled out of his office and down the hall. He smiled, wondering how much a flight to Montenegro would be.

THE END

If you were as enamored with this twisted love triangle as I was, be sure to check out the remarkable song to cap this series, *Bridges We Must Burn* written and performed by Kimberly Reszetylo.

If you've enjoyed this final chapter, your **quick spoiler-free review on Amazon** is incredibly helpful. Please and thank you!

More from J.R. Mason:
The Confessions Series:
Confessions of a Sane Single Woman
Soulmate Setbacks: Confessions II

The Pieces Series:
Stolen Pieces
Stolen Pieces II: Grave Misconduct
Stolen Pieces III: Hidden Darkness

Acknowledgments

For the contribution of their specialized knowledge that helped this creation to be more accurate and authentic, I would like to extend a heartfelt thank you to Officer Tim Depenhart, Laura McMullen, M.D., Jodi Gill, J.D., M.C.J., James Hill, and Clarence Parrish III.

To Kimberly Reszetylo (my unstable massage therapist) who is always a listening ear (and the creepy harlot who adds her own special droplets of crazy to this insanity during what are *supposed* to be my relaxing massages), I appreciate you... and this is all your fault! Lol... No author/editor duo will ever have more epic brainstorming sessions than ours – because seriously... blood is NOT a lubricant! Lol!

To my super dope beta readers – Tanisha Stewart, Eric Kovach, Laura Russell, Ellise Martin, Heather Lubay, Jennifer Haddox-Schatz, Crystal Bonner, and Kathryn Sosnak, thank you for your time and input to enhance my instability lol...

To my readers, thank you so much for supporting this madness that I said I was never doing again, but somehow it just keeps happening! I appreciate your support and reviews! No, like seriously, GO REVIEW IT!

About the Author

J.R. Mason first dipped her toes into the writing pool when she published her nonfiction Confessions Series, a self-described bad romance – *Confessions of a Sane Single Woman* and *Soulmate Setbacks: Confessions II*. Though a third Confessions book was requested, J.R. couldn't pull herself away from her dark desire to delve into a suspenseful fiction project. And now there are *three*!

Mason received her Bachelor of Arts in Journalism and Mass Communication from Cleveland State University and her Master of Arts in Advertising / Graphic Design / Public Relations from Point Park University. A full-time marketing specialist position, along with running a freelance design company, keeps her quite busy, leaving little free time for her guilty pleasures – movies and massages!

This Pittsburgh native also takes joy in playing her trumpet, kayaking, screenplay writing, travel, outdoor fires on cool nights (but not to burn people's possessions), anything with real sugar in it, and reading spicy/dark romance and psychological thrillers.

Keep up with J.R.'s latest releases:
jrenecreative.com/books

Follow me on IG & TikTok: author_j.r.mason

www.ingramcontent.com/pod-product-compliance
Lightning Source LLC
Chambersburg PA
CBHW070407120825
30977CB00012B/748